Shitshow

Chris Panatier

SOBELO BOOKS

THE UNIVERSE IS IN US

Sobelo Books

Book cover by Kristina Osborn
Edited by L.C. Marino and L.P. Hernandez

Formatted and published by Sobelo Books

ISBN (paperback): 978-1-965389-19-5
ISBN (hardcover): 978-1-965389-20-1
ISBN (ebook): 978-1-965389-18-8

First edition, 2025

Praise for Shitshow

"What starts as a ridiculous premise quickly grows into one of the most heartfelt, dynamic, and original horror novels I've read in a long time. It's fun, it's bloody, it's goopy, and it's pretty much perfectly structured. Holy shit, this was good!" — **Sam Rebelein**, Bram Stoker-nominated author of Galloway's Gospel

"SHITSHOW is a wild, short-staining ride with a heart of gold! Behind all the toilet jokes, Chris Panatier has created a delightful blend of humor, horror, and the love of family—both born and found—in a world populated by endearing Texans and set in one terrifying carnival. It's a fun fair for all lovers of the horror genre, and as quick and easy to devour as a corndog." — **Wendy N. Wagner**, author of *Girl in the Creek* and *The Deer Kings*

"SHITSHOW is a blast! I'm a sucker for dark carnival tales, and this one has just the right mix of the bizarre, the gross, and the outright horrifying. Not to mention a whole lot of heart. Chris Panatier travels deep into Lansdale country and comes back covered in Texas mud. Or at least, I hope it's just mud. I loved this book so much! — **Josh Rountree**, author of *The Unkillable Frank Lightning*

"One part supernatural whodunnit, one part tongue-in-cheek thriller, plus a generous sprinkling of bonkers humor: Panatier serves readers a funnel cake of a weird tale. Funhouse mirrors, latrine portals, and a giant spider creature? Oh my!" — **Rebecca Rowland**, Shirley Jackson Award-nominated author of *Eminence Front*

"Chris Panatier is a fecophilia Steinbeck and SHITSHOW is his Poops of Wrath, a methane-induced hallucination only a dustbowl bard could discharge. Crack this book open carefully, 'cause there's a whiff that rises up from its pages as pungently poetic as a porta potty left in the Texan sun." — **Clay McLeod Chapman**, author of *Wake Up and Open Your Eyes*

"When a Gen X sanitation worker discovers his mom, who has dementia, has gone missing, he will stop at nothing to find her. Including going down the port-a-potty that appears to have spirited her away to a carnival-themed hell realm. Plenty of fall festival fun and gross-out humor here, plus some truly disturbing torture scenes inside the Twilight Faire. Annnddd an extra special sentimental epilogue that takes the whole book to new heights. A quick, entertaining read, best accompanied by some Fireball whiskey, that will make you think twice before using portable facilities or riding any roadside carnival attractions..." — **Jess Hagemann**, author of *Headcheese* and *Mother Eating*

"Yes, SHITSHOW by Chris Panatier is the potty humor infused, absurdist romp you're expecting, but it's so much more. It's a love letter to old school horror adventures: a little bit of Stephen King, with a dash of Ray Bradbury, and a pulpy mix of Lansdale. But at its heart is a surprisingly touching exploration of the relationships we have with our elderly loved ones. This is Panatier's magic: he lures you in with carnival ride stories that twist and excite, and then when your guard is down, he socks you right in the feels. Highly recommended." — **Ryan Leslie**, author of *The Between and Colossus*

"Like any good carnival, Chris Panatier's SHITSHOW is many things at once. It's a drop-ride into the bowels of rural Texas. A tight rope act between reality and where we go when we feel our identities are being erased. A distorted mirror held to our societal obligations. A rollercoaster through every emotion a son can have for a parent. While fun as hell, this is no kiddie ride. Strap in. Because SHITSHOW will simultaneously scare the shit out of you while also making you laugh until you pee yourself. You might want to bring a mop." — **James Sabata**, author of *Caduceus*

"SHITSHOW was too crazy for Clash Books." — **Christoph Paul**, Editor-in-Chief, Clash Books

"A book about haunted port-a-potties has no business having this much heart." — **Ryan C. Bradley**, author of *Say Uncle* and *Bad Connections*

Contents

For my dad. You wanted me to call the book *Potty Time*.
Thanks for being my first reader on everything.
I love you.

Map

Central/ West Texas

Prologue

Carnival Prize

It was the biggest goddamned stuffed bunny at the whole county fair and if that didn't get Roy laid, nothing would. He practically pranced down the midway, if you could call it that, past the squirt gun game and the ring toss, the fortune teller and the duck race, between the corndog cart and the popcorn hut, soaking in the delicious glow of jealousy.

His boots crunched hay underfoot as he hustled to the funnel cake stand where Jessie sat tipsy and waiting. She'd been the one to throw down the gauntlet, so to speak, telling him that tonight was *the* night *if* he could awe her with a suitably impressive carnival trophy. It'd cost him almost seventy-five dollars in fucking beanbags, and it was near closing time, but it was about to be worth it.

He stopped short of the picnic table where she sat and stood with a big dumb grin on his face, waiting for her to look up. It took longer than it should have, but when she did, he knew he'd done it.

"Holy shit, Roy!" She jumped up and embraced the floppy-eared colossus, then spun on her heels. Her skirt flew up a bit and Roy's heart fluttered. "You, mister," she said, giving him a peck on the cheek. "You get a prize too."

With the bunny head-locked under one arm, she led him by the other through the picnic area and behind one of the big rig trailers. There in the shadows she pulled him close and smashed her lips to his face. Her mouth was warm and aggressive, with a hint of waxy-cup beer. Not believing his good fortune, Roy considered the possibility that he might have been raptured straight to Heaven.

"Hey!" yelled a burly silhouette from the end of the trailer. "Get on out of here, you two! Park's closing!"

Giggling, Jessie pulled Roy further from the twinkling lights of the fair. The rabbit bounced up and down as they raced through the shadows. Jessie turned abruptly down a long line of port-a-potties, and they darted between them. Kissing him again, she ripped Roy's shirt out from his pants and ran her hands over his chest and below his waistband.

"Get a room, you perverts!" A squad of preteens ran off giggling.

Roy pulled away and shouted after them, but Jessie jerked him back. "I'm over here."

"Sorry," he said, feeling stupid and nervous. "Little shits."

Jessie undid his belt and unzipped his pants. Roy started freezing up. He didn't want to be so exposed. Perhaps sensing this, Jessie said, "It's fun to do it where you might get caught, don't you think?"

"Uh," he stuttered. He wanted this more than anything but was letting his long-held notions of decorum spoil the moment.

"Such a choir boy. Come on."

Jessie rounded the corner and opened the door to the first latrine. "After you."

"Ugh, really?" he gave it a sniff.

"*Adventure*, Roy," she said, yanking him inside the toilet. "Doesn't smell so bad. I don't even know if this one's been used yet."

"We left the bunny outside."

"The bunny? Jesus, Roy, I'm wondering if you really want this or not. Come. Here."

She kissed him again. When she pulled off her shirt, decorum took an instant hiatus, and the fact that this was all going down in a porta-potty flew from his mind. "Holy shit," he mumbled around her lips.

"Yes, Roy. Holy shit." Jessie crouched and yanked down his Wranglers, then reached around and grabbed his butt cheeks.

"Jessie," he whispered, just as she got his undies down.

She looked up. "Yes?" Annoyance crept into her voice.

"Do you hear that?"

She cocked her head and comically cupped a hand to her ear. "Hear what, Roy?"

"In there." He pointed into the black hole of the toilet as the bit of him Jessie held in her hand shriveled up like a gas station hot dog. She stood and looked into the tank. It came again as a gurgling. Some wet, slapping noises.

Jessie waived it off. "It's ... it's just the plumbing, you know."

"I don't think these things have plumbing."

The air filled with an odor unlike anything Roy'd ever smelled. Something indescribable but akin to a wad of catfish bait crammed in a toaster. The sound changed to a hiss, followed by a rasping AHHHHHHHH and then the throaty turning of a growl.

Jessie screeched and spun toward the door. Roy, hobbled by his pants, toppled sideways, blocking the escape and tripping Jessie. "Get up!" she screamed. "Get up! Get—"

The tank rumbled violently, splashing water from the hole and shaking the entire port-o-let side to side.

Roy, tangled in his briefs and fumbling with his Wranglers, froze, his attention on the towering silhouette of the thing that loomed up from the toilet hole. Jessie twisted her neck to see. "Roy?" she said, her voice small and pleading. "Roy? What is that?"

Chapter One

Bologna

Sunday McWhorter considered serving an egg with a broken yolk among the greatest offenses one man could bring against another. Even if the man was his mother and even if she didn't much care where the yolks were in relation to the rest of the egg so long as they were present somewhere on the plate. Sunday had his standards. His eggs came out hot and with their yolks intact. He started over.

"Eggs," he said, finishing his second attempt with a sprinkle of pepper. He set the plate at his mother's spot in the kitchenette. He popped the toast and buttered it, giving each of them a slice. Dipping a corner into the broken yolks of the first batch, he took a bite. "Eggs," he called again.

His mother, Regina McWhorter, emerged from her bedroom at the good end of the singlewide, which was to say that it didn't leak as bad as the end where Sunday made his quarters. She was a tall woman and tough, too. She'd once dropped a beating on a police deputy so bad he'd quit and joined the postal service. Apparently, he'd tried turning a routine detention into a dalliance.

She was tough still, but it was the early stages of dementia and so that meant she had to live with Sunday—a fact that she didn't like when she remembered it. Sunday gave her a hug as she sat down behind a gauzy ribbon of breakfast steam. Kissing the top of her head, he felt her go stiff. She'd been doing that more lately. "You okay?"

"Hm-mm, yes, of course."

"Oop—almost forgot the Cholula," he said, fetching the hot sauce from the counter by the stove. He placed it in front of her, then expertly bound her long hair in a scrunchie so it didn't get in her yolks. Sitting back down, he put his own hair back with a second scrunchie and polished off his eggs, using the crust of his toast to scrub the plate. Swallowing, he said, "Gotta make my route this morning. I might be gone a bit longer than usual with the county fair and whatnot, but Ms. Poppy is right next door and she'll be by to check on you."

"I'll be just fine." Her smile turned suddenly bright. Even at seventy-one, her face retained its youthful sparkle. It almost made him cry, remembering the old her. Back when nothing got in her way—especially anyone who suggested the job was beyond her. She once mixed and poured an entire concrete driveway out of spite after their old next-door neighbor Bryant Childress suggested she get a man to help around the house. Afterward, she offered to pour him a new driveway, too. After that, he stopped giving Regina McWhorter advice.

Sunday reached across the little table and squeezed her hand.

"When did you get those?"

He looked down at the tattoos covering his hands and fingers.

"Had them most my life, Mom."

She pointed to a questionably rendered image of a German Shepherd beneath the logo for the band Motörhead on the meat of his forearm. "That's new."

"That's Lemmy. You don't remember him?"

"You've had so many dogs."

"Not since Lemmy." Lemmy was Sunday's favorite musician, R.I.P., and Lemmy the dog had been Sunday's favorite dog, also R.I.P.

Her eyes wandered. "I have a garden to tend. It's a sunny day."

He glanced out the window and drank down his coffee. "That it is."

Sunday waited until his mother finished her plate then took the dishes to the sink and washed them. He put a kiss on her head and lingered there, wishing there was some way to infuse her with his strength. She'd given him so much of hers. It honestly felt like a debt he'd never repay. He said goodbye.

On the way to the truck, he caught a glimpse of Poppy Johnson at her kitchen window. She waved. He pointed toward his trailer and she returned an enthusiastic thumbs up. Having Ms. Poppy next door to look after his mother was a stroke of luck he wouldn't take for granted. Sunday didn't consider himself a superstitious man. He carried around a modicum of what he believed to be the *regular default* amount of superstition for most people and so made sure to keep Ms. Poppy well-stocked in Fireball Cinnamon Whiskey, which she liked to sip on during evenings and anytime the sun was up. It was a small kindness for all she did for his mother. And he didn't mind one bit if the universe took it as an offering for continued good fortune. That wasn't a gratuitous degree of superstition in his mind, just *regular default*.

He went out to his truck and climbed in. He was shutting the door when his mother came down the steps in shorts and a t-shirt with one of his flannels hanging loosely over it. She took up her gardening gloves and caught him watching her. "I'm fine, Sunday Everett," she said, bright eyed. "You'll be late."

Another glance to Ms. Poppy in her window, who kindly gestured for him to go. He nodded and started the truck. The big diesel roared to life. He hated winding her up in the trailer park and startling everybody, but she sounded like a tornado made of hammers trapped in a metal trashcan. Sunday was a freelance wrecker by trade, but once he took over his mom's care, the twenty-four-hour on-call life didn't work anymore. He missed his old truck for a lot of reasons, but mostly because it didn't have a giant tank of sewage strapped to the back. The company permitted him to use it as his personal vehicle so long as he didn't abuse the privilege.

He backed out carefully, then shifted to first gear and slow rolled from the mobile home park. At the exit to the road, he stopped and pulled up the Monday route on his phone. There were the usual construction sites and sports complexes he'd have to hit, as well as the county fairgrounds. He rubbed his beard and thought on the order of things. Fair didn't open 'til late, so he figured to do that one last.

The honeywagon, Sunday called her Honey, presented a rather cushy ride where service vehicles were concerned, and its specs were top of the line. It had a two-chamber, twelve-hundred-gallon aluminum tank, two suction hoses, and a vacuum pump that could draw over two-hundred cubic feet of human excreta every minute. The cherry on top was a fold down carrier with room enough for two latrines. Truth be told, among drivers of portable restroom service units, Sunday had hit the jackpot. And the smell didn't even bother him anymore. Enough time spent around raw sewage will burn out the olfactories right quick.

The morning went about as well as Sunday could have expected, vacuuming out the portables at the ball fields and a handful of residential build sites. Only once did he lose suction and need to hit the shut-off valve before the backflow turned the portable into a gusher. He dug a crumpled potato chip bag out of an access port while absently lecturing would-be toilet users that this is what happens when you treat a port-a-john like a trash can. Aside from that one hitch, the morning passed pleasantly.

Pulling up to the Somervell County Fairgrounds, however, Sunday could see things were anything but *regular default*. He took Honey slowly over the uneven gravel and up beside a pop-up shade tent cordoned off in yellow police tape. A gangly officer with a planetoid of a belly marched over and Sunday rolled down the window as Honey drew to a stop.

"Fairgrounds are shut down until we're done with our sweep," said the cop, who had the profile of a chopstick stabbed through a pomegranate.

"I'm here for toilet maintenance."

"Doesn't matter what you're here for. When they're done, you can go in."

"What's going on?"

"Missing kids. Teenagers. The usual."

Sunday didn't see that it was usual at all. He couldn't remember any missing persons cases in Glen Rose and was unable off hand to recall if there'd ever been any involving teens, though now that he thought about it, such an event just *seemed* common. Or maybe that was the movies blending with real life. "Alright, but like I said, I'm just here to drain the portables."

"Yeah. I heard you. Hang here until they're done. It's the last sweep and then they're moving the search into the woods." He gestured with his head as if Sunday was blind to the massive wall of pine and red oak behind the staging area.

The officer trundled off to the sunshade where he produced a glazed donut from a white cardboard box and bit the side out of it like a shark on a life preserver.

It was another forty-five minutes before a pack of uniforms emerged from the front gate. The Donut Shark leisurely pulled aside the crime scene tape and waved Sunday through.

It dawned upon him then. In his fifty-two years he'd never been to a county fair during the day. Seeing one people-less and quiet in the broad daylight was at odds with nature. County fairs self-manifested at dusk and dissembled come dawn. But here he was.

Honey crawled over the gravel, and even though Sunday was at the helm, he sensed her hesitation. Maybe he was more anxious than he'd realized. No one expected missing teens first thing on a Monday morning. He tapped the gas to reassure himself he was still in control. Honey rumbled back that he was.

The latrines formed a meandering blue wall on the fairground's southern border, and Sunday *tsked* sadly at their sloppy placement. He pulled Honey alongside and eased her to a stop, then climbed down and got his hoses situated. In no time he'd pumped the first toilet and completed the routine cleaning. Being early in the fair's run, the units weren't overly laden, and the work went fast.

Leaning against the truck while replenishing the toilet's fresh water, Sunday gazed over the deserted fairgrounds. The midway with its trick games, the Tilt-a-Whirl, the corny-dog shack, funnel cake hut, the Zipper. He imagined the world flashing to night, the lights coming alive, people squealing like jail-broken lemurs high on whippets while getting tossed about by dodgy rides with questionable maintenance histories. He saw himself as a child leading his mother by the hand from one attraction to the next, the smile on her face aglow at the sight of his unbridled joy.

Then it was day again.

Sunday dropped a packet of blue biocide into the tank and restocked the toilet paper.

He was just about to shut the door and be done when he spotted a clutch of Harvestmen nesting up in the corner. "Oh shit," he said, grabbing his chest. Sunday wasn't a man possessed of many earthly fears, but seeing a wad of daddy longlegs scurrying for cover was about the goddamned worst thing that could happen to a person, broken yolks excepted. He got his utility hose and sprayed them out from a distance.

He went to the next portable and propped the door open with his bucket, careful to check for more of the stick-legged arachnids. Thankfully, it was all clear. A gap between units allowed a view of the forest beyond. He walked past the wall of latrines and considered the dense woods, wondering if he was being watched. It wouldn't be hard. The leaves were still on the trees and had only started changing. Turning back to his work, he nearly jumped out of his skull at a pair of giant eyeballs staring blindly from behind the unit. "Jesus hell!" he cried out, skipping backward.

The rabbit's disproportionally massive head was made of some shiny aquamarine fabric that would probably burst into flames if it got within ten feet of a spark. The eyes were like saucers, perfectly round, and attached not on the front of its face in proximity to the tiny triangle nose and whiskers, but on the sides of its head, fish like. The damned thing was an abomination—a fat old largemouth in Easter Bunny drag. The paws were stubby and poorly sewn like puffy fins. Carnival prizes were gaudy pieces of sweat shop fuckery, but this thing was unique even by that standard. He brought it back to the truck and belted it into the passenger seat, laughing at himself for getting spooked. "Bet somebody worked their ass off to win you."

He flipped on the pump and shoved the long pipe attached to the vacuum hose into the portable's tank. The machinery hummed and he let his eyes go blurry thinking about his mother again, looking for her at the fair. The idea of her. They had a rule when he was a kid: if he got lost, meet at the funhouse. He traced down the line of amusements to the end, where a pair of trailers were joined together and elaborately unfolded into something else entirely. A mind warping and mirror-filled world that went on for miles, where your fear of never getting out was what drew you there in the first place. His mother stood beside the steps and beckoned to him.

The sky turned to night. Then even darker than night. Purple black. The fair lights kindled then went out, dim and weak like dying stars. Sunday straightened, his pulse ramping up. Something churned in the earth, a low thrum vibrating through the heels of his work boots. Another sound came over the grounds through the speakers up on poles, greasy and wrong like a violin played in reverse. Back at the funhouse, his mother, still waving, retreated from view. "Mom?" *he mumbled. He tried to follow but his feet wouldn't move. The starless sky spun. The churning grew louder, grinding to an ear-splitting crescendo, a mechanical scream. Sunday clapped his hands to his ears and squeezed his eyes shut.*

The vacuum whinnied and rattled. Sunday snapped out of his night-time vision into the noon sun and ran over to kill the pump. He cursed himself for letting it run dry. Back at the tank, he saw it had hardly emptied at all. If he found another bag clogging the line he'd—well, he didn't know what he'd do—he'd be pissed.

He reversed the flow to purge the line, then checked the toilet hole and stared into the nozzle. It dribbled muddy liquid, meaning that the clog was still in the line. Back on Honey, the pump worked harder, whining as the pressure increased. Something began to emerge from the nozzle. Pale and stained blue from biocide, it was folded up like a giant, oversoaked lasagna noodle.

Then it popped clear, followed by a gush of liquid. Sunday skipped to the truck and killed the pump, then ran back inside to see what had come out. Getting shot out of a hose at over 200 PSI had plastered the object against the inside wall of the tank, giving it the appearance of a deflated bologna. A bologna with a little happy face, complete with eyes and nostril holes and a mouth cut into it. Sunday pivoted his head for better perspective and saw a mess of stringy black laying moplike over the bologna's terminus. He leaned in. "Is that hair?"

Realizing what he was looking at, Sunday let out a squeal in the register of a butt-shot raccoon and scurried backward from the toilet all the way to Honey. He climbed in, slammed the door, seized the wheel and tried not to black out.

Valera Weekly Dispatch-Times

Local Woman Reported Missing From Traveling Carnival Venue

Police Chief Melinda Hernandez said on Monday that mother of three, Georgia Harvey, was last seen at the Titan Brothers Traveling Carnival in the Sunflower Strip Center parking lot at approximately 7:30 p.m. on Tuesday night. "She left me and the kids over by the Gravitron because she didn't want to ride it," said husband Charles Harvey. "She went off for a snack and to use the bathroom. She just never came back."

Chief Hernandez stated that it was too early to label this a kidnapping case. "We're exploring all possibilities. But people wander off all the time."

Chapter Two
CHAIN OF CUSTODY

Sunday told the cops what he'd found, then suffered the great misfortune of having the Donut Shark assigned to accompany him back to the suspect portable. The man wouldn't shut up. He chattered endlessly about every goddamned thing from the state of law enforcement (too many cameras, not enough 'freedom to police') to the influx of hippies getting naked and stoned in the Paluxy River. Sunday had had enough by the time they reached the row of latrines. "It's this one," he said, directing the cop to the suspect toilet, and wishing him to maybe drown in it.

The deputy inspected the tank through the toilet hole, then gasped and shot back from it as if he'd been punched. He stumbled off balance through the dust and fell square on his rear. "Sunday, you got a human face in your port-o-let."

"I told you that. How did it get there?"

The officer rolled to one side in the way of a land-born manatee and reached into his back pocket. "Here," he said, brandishing a sheet of paper with photos of the missing teens. Sunday took it and read.

According to the poster, the girl, Jessie Kinkaid, was age twenty, though Sunday considered anyone below the age of twenty-five as basically teen-aged. The deputy got himself upright and snatched away the paper then waddled back to the portable. Turning the paper to orient the faces to the blue-stained swatch of skin in the tank, he grunted matter of fact. "Yep, I think that's the young one. The male."

"How does someone's face come off like that?" asked Sunday, trying to impress upon the officer the gravity of the situation that he didn't feel was being reciprocated.

"Looks like somebody skinned a Smurf, doesn't it?" He chuckled but quickly stifled his laughter. "Well, there's no doubt in my mind—you've got the last known remains of Roy West Carpenter here in your shitter. See here? The cleft in the chin? The Roy Orbison sideburns?"

Sunday glanced between the poster and the face, which now that he'd adjusted to it seemed less like a flattened bologna and more like uncooked pizza dough that somebody went twirling and accidentally dropped in the toilet. He hadn't noticed the sideburns, but the Donut Shark had a point. The kid had cultivated his sideburns down near to where his jawline had once been. And behind the black patches of hair, more dough and some little ear nubs. Sunday's stomach flinched a warning and he shifted himself into the breeze outside.

It was another hour of listening to the man talk before the forensics team arrived to remove Roy's face from the tank. They fished it out with a litter picker, then dropped it into a five-gallon bucket. He gave a statement while they probed the tank for evidence, then leaned on Honey and waited. As the afternoon light waned, the Donut Shark emerged from a scrum of officials to inform him that the toilet had turned up nothing else of interest. Sunday breathed a sigh of relief. Not that he didn't want them to get their evidence. He'd had enough of unclaimed body parts.

"So, look, you obviously gotta pull this one out of service," said the deputy. Over his shoulder, a pair of cops wound yellow tape around the unit.

"*You* aren't taking it? Isn't it evidence?"

The cop made an incredulous face and glanced back to the unit. "Porta potty don't fit in the evidence room."

"So, I'll take it back to Sloan Environmental."

"Hmm. Look, you know how it is. Chain of custody and whatnot. You're a witness now, Sunday." He pronounced it *Sundee*. "You're how we authenticate the toilet if it all becomes a courthouse situation." He slapped him on the shoulder like he'd been deputized, then filled out a slip of paper and shoved a clipboard into Sunday's chest. "Sign."

"What is this?"

"That's the chain of custody form."

"Do I have to sign it?"

"Don't be a pain in my ass. This unit is going home with you." He gestured to it. "Look. It's been taped up and logged right here on the form. Go ahead now."

Sunday frowned, but did as he was instructed, after which the Donut Shark said, "I hereby release said toilet into your custody for the pendency of the investigation."

"Where the hell am I supposed to store it?"

"Not really my concern. It's your responsibility now."

"What if I don't want to take it?"

"What if I didn't wake up this morning hoping to get to see a face dug out of a crapper?"

"At least let me drain it first."

"Can't do that. Evidence."

"It'll slosh everywhere and stink up the whole trailer park!"

The cop shrugged.

"You don't live there. At least let me top off the biocide."

"Nah, can't let you—"

"It won't destroy anything inside but bacteria. And it will cover the smell so that my neighbors don't kill me in the night ... or worse, try to get rid of your evidence themselves."

The deputy pursed his lips. "Yeah, fine." He marched to the crime scene and had the others unwind the yellow tape.

Sunday added water and chemicals, then duct-taped a sheet of plastic over the hole so it didn't slosh everywhere during transport. Then it was rewrapped.

The face had been shocking. There was no doubt about that, yet it was the forced stewardship of a portable toilet that had Sunday seeing red and questioning his life. Grumbling, he lowered the bumper attachment at Honey's rear and slid it under the unit. The hydraulics hoisted it to the bed and Sunday strapped it.

He climbed into the cab and turned the engine. The Donut Shark's face popped up at the window. Sunday jumped in his seat. "Jesus, what now?"

The deputy looked across to the passenger side. "What you doing with that?"

Sunday considered the fish-eyed bunny and was about to tell the story of finding it behind the toilet but had had enough of local law enforcement. "Something for my mother."

"She like rabbits, then?"

"She likes rabbits just fine."

"Everybody's got their thing, I guess," said the officer. He handed over a slip of paper. "Put this in your wallet. That's my office line. It also has the tag number for the evidence."

Sunday grinned tightly and took the card. "Anything else?"

"You planning on going to the fair?"

"Unlikely."

"I get it," he said, hopping down and sauntering off. Sunday put Honey into gear and rolled for home.

Clifton Breakfast Digest

Four Gone Missing in Church Field Trip

What was supposed to be a community-building
jaunt by members of the Sandy Hill Baptist
Church turned tragic Sunday night, says
Pastor Albert Woods. Two adults and two
children from the group have been reported
missing from the Bosque County Livestock
Show and Haunted Forest. "It's in the middle
of a field surrounded by hay bales. Nobody
saw anyone they didn't know. We're all just
so confused."

Chapter Three

Scissors

S unday was in a sour mood when he backed Honey into the gravel beside the singlewide of Lot 11. Normally, he'd be inside and washed up, cooking dinner for Mom and sometimes Ms. Poppy, but now he had to stow a piece of state's evidence in the side yard. It was five minutes before he got it down and shimmied into place. Panting and sweating, he realized the toilet blocked the only window in his bedroom. Cursing under his breath, he opened Honey and yanked out the bunny, then made for the house.

Ms. Poppy waved to him when he opened the front door. "Hey Sunday." Her old voice had the strain of someone getting up from the couch even when she wasn't moving. She eyed the rabbit. "Hell you got there?"

"Hey Ms. Poppy, where is she?"

"Sleepin'. She had a rough afternoon. Is that a—that a carnival prize?"

Sunday drifted to the door to her bedroom just to feel proximate. "She okay?"

"Nothing we haven't seen before. Just longer episodes when it comes. Disease is getting deeper. That's all."

Sunday eyed the column of sticky notes his mother had put on the wall. WATER YOUR GARDEN EVERY MORNING. REMEMBER TO SHOWER. THE MAN LIVING IN THE TRAILER WITH YOU IS YOUR SON. YOU ARE ALLERGIC TO CRAWDADS.

Even when the doctors explained the diagnosis, even when the medication made her symptoms worse, it was hard to accept what was happening. He knew the tire was rolling down the hill and that it'd only go faster. Dementia was a damned cruel hell. How does a person's mind simply disintegrate? He dropped down at the end of the couch close to where Ms. Poppy sat in the kitchenette and plopped the bunny beside him, a fish-eyed wingman. "What happened?"

Ms. Poppy was a tiny woman with tiny eyes. Small enough that a single tear would fill them completely. Her black hair was striped in grey and pulled hard into a bun away from her acorn-brown face. Sunday wondered if her forehead had always been so big or if she'd just persuaded the hair backward from its original spot. She flicked at her lighter with one of her squirrel-like paws. Ms. Poppy smoked cigars. Big, cheap, flavored cigars from wherever she could get them: the gas station, the liquor store. It didn't matter so long as it put off thick, yellow smoke. She abstained when inside his trailer, of course, but the constant flicking was the clear reminder of what was to come as soon as she left. Convenience store cigars and Fireball Cinnamon Whiskey and staying up all night, because as far as Sunday knew, Ms. Poppy didn't sleep or eat food.

She cleared her throat. "Oh, you know. She forgets and blames herself. She went looking through the cabinets again."

Sunday hadn't even noticed the state of the place when he'd come in. Maybe the day had worn on him more than he'd realized. Ms. Poppy had closed most of the cabinet doors except the high ones his mom could reach but that Ms. Poppy couldn't. Sunday stood and quietly shut them.

"I'm sorry," he said. "I'm sorry you had to be here for it."

"I been here for it plenty. It was just worse today."

"Usually means it'll be better tomorrow. It's always better the next day."

Ms. Poppy flicked her lighter. "Until it isn't."

Sunday went to the fridge and flicked a piece of masking tape on the door that read *DON'T EAT THE CRAWDADS*. "I have chili, and I have ..." he said, opening the door, "well, just chili. Can I heat you up a bowl?"

The old woman waved her hand and grunted up from the table. "No, no. I've got dinner waiting for me over in mine."

"Whiskey ain't dinner, Ms. Poppy."

"It is if you put it over ice."

She made him smile even though he wasn't in a smiling mood. "You got any actual food over there?"

"Got all I need." She got on her tiptoes to put a kiss on his cheek and left him standing inside the fridge. "You get some rest." Then she drifted out the door like a willow leaf.

Sunday went to his mother's door and listened until he keyed on her respirations, probably like how a new parent sneaks in to make sure their newborn is still breathing. He heated the leftover chili in the microwave and poured it over some Fritos, not even taking time to grate cheese. Such was the day.

Sunday perked from his pillow and listened. The trailer park was full of noises, so he was used to it, but it wasn't outside noises that concerned him. He kept his head up and waited until he heard the unmistakable sound of squeaking hinges. Riffling through cabinets wasn't his mother's typical nightly habit. He crawled from bed and opened his door.

Moonlight poured through the blinds, illuminating the bone-studded curve of his mother's naked back, her head buried in a cabinet below the counter. Pots and pans clanged and shuffled as she rummaged. He didn't want to give her a start, so he waited, but he hated that she was unclothed. The chilly October air didn't respect the walls of the singlewide.

After a few seconds, the cabinet went quiet and she retreated on all fours, her breasts dusty from their journey across the floor. She twisted her head, black eyes twinkling. She said, "It's you, isn't it?"

"It's me, Ma."

"You're him, aren't you?"

He took a blanket from the couch and draped it over her, then helped her stand and embraced her. "I'm Sunday, your son, Mom."

"You called to me. You told me to check the drawers and cabinets again."

"Mom, I didn't."

She pushed away and glared hard. "Who was it, then?"

"I don't know. Let's try to get some sleep, okay?"

He led her back into her room and yanked her nightgown from where she'd tossed it over the bar holding up the curtains up. "Arms high," he said, slipping it back on. "Don't take your clothes off like that. It's getting cold now, okay?" She nodded and crawled into bed when he opened the blankets for her. He sat on the edge and rubbed her arm. "There's nothing in those cabinets but kitchenware and rat bait, Mom. What you're looking for ... it's not there. It's not anywhere. You understand?"

She stared up at the ceiling, humming lightly. Sunday tucked the sheets tight around her, then left. As the door closed, she said, "You told me I'd need a knife."

"I did what?"

She hummed again.

"Mom, what? I didn't tell you anything about a knife."

Her eyes went distant and she continued humming like her mind was on commercial break. She was on to the next thing and the previous thing was now fading in the background.

"I love you, Mom. Goodnight."

"Love you too, my darling."

He left the door open and went to the kitchen where he gathered all the knives, then hid them away in his bedroom closet. Sitting on his bed, he confronted the reality of her disease. They didn't have much. She had Social Security and Medicare. In the morning he'd call her physician for an evaluation, a referral for ... he didn't know. A home nurse? Long-term care? He laid back and allowed his eyes to wander over the popcorn ceiling in search of patterns. The only thing he saw before drifting to sleep was a colossal big top circus tent, turning slow like a Lazy Susan.

Regina heard it again, calling to her just as before. Only this time she realized Sunday was right. It wasn't his voice at all. It was a higher power. She fought free of the sheets and shuffled into the living room. Sunday snored in his bed at the other end of the house. The voice said to be quiet, that it was essential that Sunday not be wakened. She tip-toed into the kitchenette and allowed her eyes to settle on the stuffed bunny watching her from the couch. "It's you," she whispered.

"It's me," said the rabbit with the power of its mind.

She came closer. "Will I still need a knife to find what is lost?"

"Yes," said the rabbit, its happy expression unchanging. "But your son hid them all in his closet."

"What will I do!"

"Shhhhhh," it said. "What about scissors?

"Ah, yes!" She went to a drawer of Sunday's junk.

"Silence is of utmost importance if you want to find what is lost."

Regina appreciated the warning. She did very much want to find what was lost. She searched through the drawer, delicately lifting screwdrivers and fishing line and eyeglass repair kits and batteries until the scissors appeared. Nice big ones. Good for cutting what had to be cut. She held them up to the bunny.

"Goooooood," it said. Then she walked from the kitchenette to stand in Sunday's doorway, scissors gleaming in the moonlight.

The Jones County
Community News

Anson High Football Skipper Disappears from Competitive Gourd Sculpting Event

ANSON - Beloved teacher and Anson High varsity football coach Vance Read has been missing since Thursday Night, when he was seen at the pumpkin carving contest at the Jones County Fall Festival. His family has asked anyone with knowledge of his whereabouts to contact local authorities. Citizens can also call the Community News anonymous tip-line.

Chapter Four

Hasenpfeffer

I t was bright outside when Sunday woke. His face was wet. Startled, he shot up and touched his cheek, pulling away a fat string of drool. He looked down the length of the singlewide to his mother's room. Door wide open. Bed empty.

He launched himself out of bed and through to the other side of the trailer. No one home. Still with his boots on from the day before, he crashed out the front door. His watch said half past nine. How the hell did she get out without him hearing? Running to Ms. Poppy's, he bellowed across the neighborhood. Ms. Poppy emerged in her robe with questions on her face and a smoking cigar between her fingers. "She ran off?"

"Dunno!"

"You go check the loop and I'll scooter over to the front, see what's to see." Ms. Poppy mounted her Rascal Scooter like it was a Harley and gave herself whiplash taking off. Her robes rippled as she raced down the drive. Sunday ran as best as he could down the main road, which was just a big circle, calling for Mom, calling for Regina McWhorter.

By the halfway point he was panting hard and a stitch stabbed at his ribcage. He'd been carrying an extra twelve pack, maybe a case over the top of his belt buckle and he just couldn't keep up. Slowing to a trot, he continued around as neighbors came out to offer help, and soon the entire under-employed segment of Live Oaks Enclave was in on the search.

Sunday dialed 9-1-1 then hung up before it started ringing. Better to call someone he knew, even if the deputy was annoying as hell. Sunday felt he was owed one on account of the evidence storage and saving the man on paperwork. Maybe a personal connection would boost the search effort. He dug into his wallet for the Donut Shark's number and made the call.

He headed back to Lot 11 to wait for the officer, who, according to the card, had a name. It was Gaynes. Edward Garp Gaynes. Ms. Poppy was there already, shaking her head. "Nothing out front."

He stopped dead in the road. Slowly, he stepped backward until the porta potty came into full view, out from Honey's backside. "Ms. Poppy!"

"Sunday?"

He rushed to the portable. "Did you see anyone, ANYONE, come over here?"

"Nobody."

The yellow police tape had been cut along the line of the door. Scissors from his junk drawer laid on the ground. He swallowed and turned the latch, unready to see what had happened inside. He threw the door open.

Nothing. No mess. No human remnants. But the plastic over the hole was torn away. He shoved his head inside, terrified he might see his mom's eyeless mask staring back.

Ms. Poppy rolled up on her Rascal. "What is it?"

Confusion clogged his brain like a wad of candy wrappers in Honey's vacuum line as he studied the glassy surface of the water inside the tank. His mom had broken into the portable toilet for some reason. Certainly not to use it, right? Though these days he could hardly write off any of her behavior as atypical. He shut the door and backed way, picking up the scissors and pocketing them. He was breathing too hard. Hyperventilating. His heart thumped like Lemmy Kilmister's big bass guitar intro on *Overnight Sensation*.

The morning sky flashed to night, the purple-black of a fearful place Sunday didn't want to know. "Do you see this?" he asked. "Ms. Poppy?" He turned to where she'd been sitting on her scooter. She wasn't there.

The latch on the portable turned slowly and clicked open. Sunday backed away as the door opened of its own accord, giving the unit a cavernous black mouth. Then a smile appeared inside, widening with teeth glowing yellow, and above it, two points of light. She came to stand at the threshold of the black with her hand outstretched, fingers rolling a summoning request.

"*Mom, come on out of there,*" *said Sunday. She shook her head side to side in slow motion, her long hair dragging wet over her sopping robin's egg gown. He held his hand out and beckoned.* "*Let's go inside.*"

She turned and walked back into the portable's ever deepening maw. Sunday cried out and ran for her.

He clocked the door with his face.

"Sunday?" said Ms. Poppy, rolling closer. "You alright?"

He rubbed his forehead. "One of my visions."

"You get visions? I had a cousin who got visions. Ended up trying to raise cheese goats."

"Look at it!" Sunday exclaimed, holding his arms open to portable. "It's just another cabinet, Ms. Poppy. She went looking for what was lost."

"You think she's in there?"

"I don't know a goddamned thing, Ms. Poppy. I need to think."

"Don't let me stop you."

"Do you have tape?"

"Tape?"

"Tape! To tape things together."

"I got gift tape."

"Yes. Fine. Please."

"Don't have to ask me twice," said Ms. Poppy.

"Not a word about this, okay?"

She backed her Rascal up and turned for her driveway. "A word about what? That you think your mom blew town through a port-a-potty? Don't have to worry about me regaling anyone with that story, Sunday McWhorter."

She came back with a dispenser of Scotch tape, then rolled out to the street. Sunday quickly went to mending the police tape so it seemed intact, at least from afar.

"Police are on their way," said Ms. Poppy before driving off in a cloud of grape-smelling cigar smoke.

A pair of Glen Rose Police Department cruisers rolled up in front of his home and parked. The Donut Shark, Deputy Gaynes, got out. "Never saw you before yesterday, now it's two days in a row?"

Sunday's face must have warned the deputy off any further pleasantries, Deputy Gaynes cleared his throat and continued. "So, we've got a missing mother. I already put out an APB. County and State have it too. If she turns up anywhere about town, we'll know."

Sunday filled out a form on a clipboard that Gaynes provided and answered basic questions, explaining that his mother had early—was it still early anymore?—dementia.

"Had a touch of it in my family too." He stretched his head to look over at the porta-potty sitting in the shadow of the singlewide, then pushed close into Sunday's personal space with breath like breakfast. "Hey, listen to this. It's not exactly public yet, but two more have gone missing since last night. Separate incidents. One in Bosque County, one in Jones. Both taken from their respective County Fairs. You believe that shit? What are the odds?"

"Just worried about my mom right now."

"No where's safe anymore. It's like I always say." Except he didn't say anything further. Sunday side-eyed him. "Anyway, I'll let you know if we hear anything," he concluded, giving him a tentative pat on the shoulder.

Sunday crisscrossed Glen Rose and the outlying areas. He didn't know why. He didn't expect to find his mom walking the main roads. It was a gesture. A thing you did when someone goes missing. Like putting up posters for a lost cat. A gesture. Then he wondered if cats were ever really lost or if they just decided to move on when they got tired of a place. It made him linger on the possibility that she'd gone away because she wanted to, because she'd lost her freedom and felt trapped with him in the singlewide.

Sunday pulled into the parking lot of the Catfish Parlor, turned off the truck, and checked in with Ms. Poppy. No news.

He sat with his thoughts while Honey's engine ticked the heat away, watching the early dinner crowd flowing inside for the Parlor's famous all-you-can-eat hushpuppies. His brain had a habit of noticing what his eyes didn't, always spinning like a top in perpetual motion. Over the years he'd learned that his subconscious brain was a harder worker than his waking mind, and it often pointed to answers and associations his front-facing self didn't grab hold of. Because about right now something was eating at him.

Gaynes had mentioned people missing in both Bosque and Jones Counties. He brought up his phone and typed a search on its cracked-ass screen (broken on the first day he got it, a record). *Kidnappings+Bosque County+Jones County+Fairs*

An article from the *Stephenville A.M. Record* was the first result. "But Stephenville's in Erath County," he mumbled. And a big city compared with the frontier hamlets that made Jones and Bosque. He began to read.

STEPHENVILLE A.M. RECORD

Thirteen Now Missing Across Six Counties in Autumn Amusements Kidnapping Spree

By Gracie McCallister, Law Correspondent

The latest in a rash of missing persons reports comes from Comanche County in the unincorporated town of Proctor, where a thirty-three-year-old pie eating contestant identified as Bradley Svach, heir to Central Texas Kolache King Josef Svach, disappeared before the competition could begin. He had reported going to visit the facilities and wasn't seen again.

Authorities have withheld details regarding possible suspects, though multiple witnesses, perhaps captivated by the spirit of the season, have provided unverified descriptions of the culprit. From a hulking creature of simian proportions to a roving gang of halfling goblins. Officials have denied these accounts outright.

The disappearance of Svach brings the total number of missing persons to thirteen across Comanche (Proctor), Erath (Stephenville), Jones (Anson), Bosque (Clifton), Coleman (Valera), and Somervell Counties (Glen Rose).

"Fourteen," mumbled Sunday. "Fourteen missing persons."

He dug into the glove compartment for his Texas roadmap and laid it across the steering wheel. Flipping the cap from a ballpoint, he circled the places named in the article: Glen Rose, Stephenville to the west. Then Clifton, Valera, Anson, and Proctor. Drawing an unsteady line from one to the next, he waited for his mind to make connections that would bring it all together like happens in police shows, but it remained blank. He dialed Ms. Poppy again. Still no sign of Mom.

He played out the scenario in which his mother was gone for good. What if? Sunday hated contemplating the eventuality, but he didn't push it away even as his thoughts went dark. If she disappeared, he wouldn't have to worry anymore. Wouldn't have to constantly fetch her from people's yards as she tended to flowers that weren't hers. Wouldn't have to hide the knives. Wouldn't have to drive a shit-wagon anymore. He punched his thigh. "You fuckin' asshole."

Driving home, Sunday couldn't shake the thought that she was no longer here. Not dead—he didn't feel that at all, strangely—just not *here*. It was a downright idiotic notion, but he kept coming back to it. No doubt, there was a connection between the other disappearances and his mother. She wasn't kidnapped from his trailer. This was something else. A disappeared cat. *Disappeared.* Not lost. And he was going to find her.

Ms. Poppy sat side-saddle in her Rascal Scooter next to the portable toilet in a cloud of cigar smoke like she'd just been summoned via incantation.

The yellow fog hung in the dead still air like a protective envelope that made her invisible to mortals. Except Sunday could see her. The smoke dissipated when Honey's blocky nose pushed a gust of air toward the singlewide.

"Nothing?" he asked, hopping out.

"Been sitting here all day," she said loosely, tapping the rim of a plastic tumbler that Sunday knew was full to the brim with Fireball on ice. "Sorry, darlin'."

He walked over and inspected the police tape. "You didn't have to sit out here all day."

"I usually sit over there all day," she said, cigar pointing to her steps. "Change of scenery. Plus, I spotted those scuzzbucket crumb-snatchers eyeballing the evidence."

Jim and Charlene Doucet had produced four largely feral children who roamed Live Oaks Enclave unsupervised, and who had not in their short lives learned to accept or acknowledge the concept of personal property. One could argue (and Sunday did) that they were waging active war against it.

"Thanks Ms. Poppy. I'm here now. You can retire for the day."

"I'll retire when I'm ready. You okay? You want to talk?"

"Think I'll just go inside and sit, and think, maybe for a bit."

"Good. Don't forget to eat."

"Sure," he said, heading up the steps.

The linoleum in the kitchenette creaked beneath his work boots. Had it always creaked like that or had he simply never noticed, with all his attention focused on his mom? It was quiet now. Like a vacuum. Like outer space.

There wasn't much food in the fridge but there was Shiner. He sat on the padded bench and flattened the Texas roadmap on the table, using the beer to hold down a corner. He took up a nearby hair scrunchie, sniffed it to remind himself of his mother's shampoo, and tied his hair up with the hot-pink band.

Staring at the line of ink he'd traced between the towns, he waited for a pattern to appear. The visual remained static, uninformative. He wasn't a student of criminal behavior or forensics but knew from TV that there was always a pattern, answers to be gleaned from innocuous clues that pointed right to the culprit. All Sunday had was the blob he'd drawn, and it seemed determined to stay that way. He drank down the beer with an easy pull and got himself two more to help limber up his neurons.

He took the beers to the little window in his room and studied the portable outside. Something had imbued it with mystical powers. Probably whatever had come for the teens and then got his mom. Leaving an empty bottle on the sill, he went back to the kitchenette and slumped onto the bench. His eyes blurred as he sipped on the third Shiner, only to have his gaze met.

The stuffed rabbit leaned against the couch cushions, its lopsided eyes staring to either side of the room but still *seeing* him.

"Mind your own business."

The rabbit didn't respond, of course, but seemed to regard him. It *paid attention*.

"You know exactly what's going on, I bet. Goddamned carnival prize."

The rabbit remained still.

"You plan this? Get together with all your buddies in Stephenville and Proctor and Valera? Hatch a kidnap and ransom scheme? Tired of being treated like objects and then discarded after two days? Figure to get your revenge against the midway gamers?" He huffed a chuckle as if he'd really let the rabbit have it. It failed to retort, but this silence felt intentional.

"You were there with the missing teens. Maybe you saw it." He leaned forward, burrowing his gaze into the dumb bunny's fat head. "Maybe ..." he drained the third Shiner, "...maybe you know exactly what's going on and you took my mother too."

The head slowly angled upright. Sunday gasped as the face squared one of its eyes to him. With no forethought, he leapt from the table, screeching like a redneck jumping wake on a jet ski, and took the rabbit by the neck, bunching air into its head. "Where is she, you bitch?"

"Everything okay in there?" called Ms. Poppy from the other side of the wall.

"Just fine! Sorry Ms. Poppy." Then, refocusing on the rabbit and twisting the oven knob to BROIL, he said, "You got one chance to tell me where she is."

He held the bunny at arm's length. Its expression remained unchanged in a defiant sort of way. "I want my mother back." He opened the oven to a wave of heat. "Last chance."

When the rabbit failed to answer, he chunked it inside, then slammed the door. The heating elements glowed orange and the bunny began to shrivel. Synthetic fabric shrank over the contours of cheap, foam pellet stuffing, drawing it tight until it resembled a gangly string of misshapen sausages in aqua green. Holes opened in the skin, rimmed in black, expanding out and dumping the stuffing onto the blazing element below. The skin gathered and pilled, melting in long strings from the rack, then caught fire. The bulbous eyes pulled together until they found Sunday through the grease-stained window, then erupted in flames.

Sunday snapped the oven off, watched as the fire devoured the last bit of oxygen inside, then opened the oven. Acrid smoke boiled out, burning his eyes and stripping away the mucous of his throat. Blindly, he ran to the window and cranked it open, stumbled to the front door and propped it. There was no worry about any fire alarm going off, he didn't have one.

Sunday stood in the gravel and coughed until his lungs were ground chuck. When the air cleared, he proceeded inside and peered in through the oven window. The rabbit's remains were a charred black husk, twisted around and intermingled with the rack like a roast overcooked by a dozen years. Rather than trying to scrape the rack clean, he removed it from the oven and tossed it out the front door.

Chapter Five

Geocache

Sunday's phone rang. He picked it up.

"Sunday, that you?" It was the Donut Shark.

"Did you find her?"

"Sorry, no."

"What, then?"

"Two new reports. One in Waco, one in Cisco. It'll be in the papers tomorrow. Both times, they found personal effects inside port-o-lets. Nothing of value. Naturally, we're operating under the presumption that these cases are toilet related. Working hypothesis is a kidnapping ring drugging folks then robbing them in the portables then smuggling them out when no one is looking. Pretty sly if you ask me."

"Why are you telling me this?"

"Well because if we're right, it means your mother's disappearance isn't connected. She's probably out for a wander."

"But all your people are searching for her, right?"

"Yeah, but it's not like we know where to look."

"Everywhere!" Sunday sighed. "Sorry. I'm uh ... I gotta go back out there and find her."

"Yeah, sure. I'll check in with you tom—"

Sunday hung up and stuffed the phone into his pocket.

He exited his trailer and marched past the rabbit-crusted oven rack and Ms. Poppy dozing in her Rascal, then climbed into Honey. She sat up when he turned over the engine.

He stuck his head out of the window. "Just running to the store, Ms. Poppy. You need anything?"

She raised up her tumbler and wiggled it side to side.

"I'm not going to that type of store just now, Ms. Poppy, sorry."

She waved him off.

Sunday didn't usually feel the compulsion to speed, but today he did, kicking up a rooster tail of dust as Honey hopped the asphalt to Highway 67. He'd cursed the day they got a Walmart, vowing to never go so long as he lived. Damned thing was a sun-scorched eyesore that they'd bulldozed ten acres of bluebonnets and thistle to build. Now, though, his personal grievances would take a back seat. He turned off the road and parked diagonally across six spots because it was faster than doing it right.

Inside, he stomped toward the wall of televisions tiled along the back, past computers and speakers and technologies he frankly didn't recognize. A sales associate yelped when he came barreling around a corner. She was a teen, about the size of Ms. Poppy.

"Oh, no! Didn't mean to startle you."

"That's alright," she said, checking herself over. "Um, can I help you?"

"Trying to find my mom."

She crinkled her forehead. "Okay. Do you need me to get on the intercom? I can call her."

"No, uh, she's not here in the store." He shook his head, trying to rid himself of the haunting vision of the slow turning big top on his ceiling playing incessantly in his mind. "She's lost. We're looking for her. She's got ... memory problems."

"That's terrible. Have you called the police?"

"Of course." He looked up to see if the ceiling had gone purple or turned into a circus tent.

"Sir?" she said, snapping his trance. "Do you need help finding something from Wal-Mart?"

Sunday relocated the teen and maintained eye contact to avoid thoughts of the circus. "I don't know what you'd call them. Do you have, like, tracers?"

"Tracerrrrrrs?"

"Like ..." He pivoted his head, looking around for something he wouldn't recognize if he saw one. "Um, in movies they put them on cars and then someone else can follow them with a computer, through satellites maybe?"

Her face lit up. "Oh, you mean like geotags?"

"Geotags?"

"You drop one in your luggage or purse, whatever, and you track it on your phone. If it gets stolen, I mean."

"Yes! You have those?"

"Sure do."

They were small and not like he'd expected, which was more something like little black boxes with blinking lights and antennae. These were little round buggers that you linked to your phone via digital application. Still, he'd found what he needed. A small victory.

Sunday thanked the teen and bought ten, then trotted back to Honey as dusk fell, tossing the bag into the passenger seat then gunning for home. Ms. Poppy was still comatose on her Rascal beside the portable. Sunday nudged her awake, then helped her into her trailer and the orange couch with floral print she called her bed.

Back in the singlewide, he unwrapped the geotags and downloaded the required phone app, to pair them via Bluetooth. Hope kindled as little green circles populated onto his phone screen. He placed the tags atop the circled cities on his Texas map. Each step felt significant, like peeling away the layers of a mystery. There was something here. It didn't want to be found out, but he was on its scent. Whatever the pattern was, he would solve it. Then he'd go save his mom, wherever she was.

He turned on the porch light and dragged an extension cord to the portable. The unit sat there, looming, putting off sinister vibes like a clown in a candy van. The air crackled with energy, enough to make Sunday's hair stand up. Or maybe it was no more than his own giddy anticipation. He stood before it, cord and caged safety lamp in hand, wondering what waited inside. A mouth of infinite black? A face-ripping maniac? Some sign of his mother? Would she call to him from the tank?

Switching on the safety lamp and holding his breath, Sunday threw open the door and washed the interior with light.

It was normal. *Regular default.* He hung the lamp by its hook and propped the door with an old tire from a truck he didn't own anymore.

Back in the toilet, Sunday made some preliminary evaluations. He tested the depth of the tank with a branch, wondering if there was a mystical quality that made it infinitely deep, like Alice's looking glass. The tip thumped the bottom of the tank, so he tossed it into the yard. He ran back inside and returned with one of the geotags, made sure it registered on his phone screen, and dropped it into the tank. *Blib.*

The green circle geolocated to within twenty yards of his home. He stared at the screen, willing it to move, to show him the path his mother had taken. But his mind quickly sobered. Is that what he'd really expect-ed? For the tag to leave the tank of the portable and go for a ride?

Instead, it did exactly what he should have expected it to do.

Fuck all.

Chapter Six

Dublin, Texas

Sunday spent the rest of the night driving around town at twenty mph. His mom, in her blue gown was everywhere, beckoning, half-glimpsed, behind a tree, only to disappear like vapor or turn away before he saw her face. He called from the open window. She never came. Once he saw her in the rearview, standing between the cab and the storage tank, hands on the back window, smiling like she did before. Before she was sick. Like in pictures from before he was born. He'd just about shit his britches but didn't turn around to check. If she was there he would have felt her.

Hours later, he pulled back in at home exhausted, throat raw and eyes crackling dry. The engine was barely off before he was asleep right there in Honey's cab.

A hail of gravel on the window woke him with the sun already over the trees. He pushed up in his seat as one of the Doucets cocked its arm with another load of rocks. Sunday elbowed the door and tumbled from Honey yelling a stream of vague and nonsensical threats as the pack of crumb snatchers scattered like coyotes.

He rounded Honey and checked inside the singlewide with a chest full of false hope. Maybe his mother had come home in the night. But inside was just as he'd left it, light on and with the map spread on the table, geotags marking each town touched by the ghosting epidemic. He remembered the geotag he'd dropped inside the portable and went outside while bringing up the tracking app on his phone.

He kicked something on the ground and stumbled over the oven rack he'd previously tossed outside. Grunting, he kicked it again, flipping it end over end into a patch of torpedo grass. A glob of residue soiled his boots. "Aw, Jesus, shit-dicks."

He grabbed a stick of mesquite and tried scraping it away, but rather than come off on the stick, it stretched longer, winding itself around his boot. "What the?" It tightened as he pried, spiraling further up his ankle and sinking into the shaft of his boot like a cable. The thing constricted, snapping the mesquite and splitting the leather of his boot. "Oh no," he said, dropping to his butt and trying to pull it off with his fingers.

It tightened further, squeezing through layers of padding and fabric, until it found skin. Sunday howled as the serpentine remnant lengthened, twining around his ankle and calf. It spiraled hot up his leg like a greasy black eel, searing through skin and flesh. He flopped backward to the dirt and weeds with a howl, writhing like bait on a hook.

When his adrenaline kicked in, he sat forward into the bar-b-que smoke of his lower leg and tried once more to extract the parasite. It was red hot to the touch. Maybe it was a trick of the mind-warping pain, but the thing seemed to breathe, its middle slowly expanding and contracting.

"What in the Devil's flat hell?" He dug his phone out to call emergency services but hesitated. What qualified the county's medical personnel to handle the malevolent possession of former carnival trophies post cremation?

That, and he didn't have time. So long as his leg still worked, he figured to power through. Lemmy would. Besides, the eel seemed to have cauterized any wounds.

He stood gingerly and tested his leg to see if it could still hold weight, then, wincing, peeled away the section of his boot which had been spiral-sliced and lowered his jeans over the evidence.

He limped to the portable. The door was open like he'd left it. The app showed the green circle for the geotag still in the tank. He stepped inside and watched the app light up. Something was happening. The green circle was there on the screen, only now it was located in Dublin.

Dublin, Texas.

Pinching the display expanded the view, showing the broader region. Stephenville, Glen Rose, Clifton, Proctor, Waco and the others.

He stormed inside, found a ruler in his junk drawer, then cleared the geotags from the map on the table. He set the straightedge across Dublin and twisted it like a propeller, stopping when the edge hit Stephenville and traced his eyes down the line. It ran straight through Proctor. Twisting again with Dublin as the hub made a line from Anson to Clifton. Then Valera to Glen Rose. Waco to Cisco. Eight towns forming the circumference of the blob he'd drawn with Dublin at the center of everything.

Now what were the odds of that as random happenstance? Lower than finding good Mexican food anywhere north of Dallas, that was for sure. This was connected. It was all connected. And the portable toilet sitting outside was a part of the equation.

Focused on the app, he grunted as he hobbled down his steps and into Ms. Poppy's front wheel. "Christ!" The woman had a Maiarian ability to materialize out of thin air.

"Anything?" she said.

"Hmm. Maybe?"

"Maybe?"

"Experiments."

"Science experiments?"

"Gotta go to Dublin. Maybe stop in Stephenville along the way. You okay here?"

"You always ask that like you're leaving me on a mountain to go find help. I'm fine. I live here."

"Yeah. Sorry."

"Could use some more go-go-juice."

"Bit early for that, don't you think?"

"For later."

He grinned and went to the passenger side of the truck, reached in through the window and pulled out a plastic bag. "Picked this up last night. Go easy, eh?"

"Love you more than my own kids," said Ms. Poppy hefting the bottle-shaped bag into her Rascal's basket.

"You never told me you had kids."

"My point."

"Well, I guess so," said Sunday, climbing into Honey's cab. "Dublin's an hour. I won't be late."

He drove out to Stephenville first. It was the closest city to Glen Rose with a disappearance and it was on the way to Dublin. He absentmindedly pressed play on Honey's compact disc player. There was only one CD in the truck, Motorhead's eponymous 1977 album *Motorhead*. He punched STOP as soon as the opening bass line came in. Music didn't feel right. He should have known better, and now he felt guilty. His mother was wandering about somewhere, probably not knowing where she was or who she was. Barefoot. Cold. Filthy. Hungry. And here he was, craving music.

He pushed down on the accelerator and Honey roared.

Stephenville was the big city, in rural Texas terms, and it took him a good thirty minutes to locate the Erath County Fair, after which he circled until he found his way in. There wasn't a police presence like in Somervell County, but then again, the victims had gone missing two days before. As for now, it was business as usual.

A fair worker flagged Sunday down, an old boy whose hat brim was wide enough to shade the entirety of the King Ranch. He sauntered over, little clouds of dust kicking up from his heels. "You here for toilets? Cause they've already been cleaned out."

"Yeah, well, that was Pete, the owner's kid, and we just found out he wasn't topping off the tanks," said Sunday, laying out the smooth line of bullshit with ease. "I'm not evacuating, just filling. Won't be long."

"Oh hell, there's nothing worse than nepotism," said the man. "My son once asked me to get him a job, and I said join the army. He did. Died in Desert Storm, rest his soul, but he achieved it all on his own. Can't take that away from him."

"Yeah," said Sunday. He touched the gas and crawled Honey to the back where the portables were set up. He undid the fill hose and got out a bucket so everything looked *regular default*, then prepped the second geotag and tried to decide which portable to use.

None had been removed from service, or if one had been, they'd replaced it. It could be any of them. Or all of them. *What would Lemmy do?* Sunday sometimes asked himself that question, but the cold truth was that Lemmy wouldn't be sucking shit out of portable latrines for his day job. Sunday opened the door to the first one and tossed the geotag into the tank, then let the door slam and focused on the tracking app.

Nothing.

He mumbled and kicked some gravel, then stepped inside the portable and gazed into the tank. Checked the app again. The green dot had settled in Dublin. Instantly.

"Okay just a second."

Back in Glen Rose the geotag hadn't moved until he'd stepped inside the unit. Same here. Gazing down at his feet, he stepped in and out a few times, trying to understand. Then he saw it, clear as a bean in chili, the residue eel from the cooked rabbit, coiled up his calf. That had to be it, right?

He went down the row to another portable and tossed an extra geotag into the tank. No movement on the app. Eyes on the screen, he stepped inside, first with his normal leg, then with the afflicted one. The tag jumped straight to Dublin.

"Ffffff."

He jumped in the truck and drove to Dublin.

Though it looked like most any other small Texas town, Dublin had specific notoriety. The town was home to Dublin Bottling Works, which for many years bottled the soft drink most beloved to Texans: Dr Pepper. Famously, they used only pure cane sugar in their batches, which gave the soft drink a natural, sweet taste. When the corporate shills over in Waco demanded they switch to corn syrup, they flipped them the bird like true heroes of the republic. The lawsuits came and Dublin Bottling Works went down swinging.

Unable to make or sell Dr Pepper by legal decree, DBW formulated "1891 Dublin Red Cola." It tasted suspiciously (exactly) like the pure cane sugar Dr Pepper recipe and wore the date of the first year Dr Pepper had been made there. It was a legendary move amongst lovers of the drink, and a brazen flaunting of the powers from which Texans pulled a substantial portion of their identity going all the way back to the state's attempt to secede from the Union in the 1860s. Of course, that had been over slavery. The state's independent streak wasn't always about sweeteners.

Sunday rolled toward Dublin on Patrick Street and even before he passed the Sonic Drive-In and the old Dublin Donuts welcoming him to town, he knew something was up because the sky was all wrong. Or, not wrong, just slightly more purple than normal.

Going by the Dairy Queen and the live bait store, people seemed not to notice the sky's strange tint, or if they did, they weren't giving any clues about it. Downtown was sleepy, with most of the old shops closed or for sale as was the usual of downtowns in the state's smaller waypoints, Glen Rose not excepted.

He stopped at Highway 6 just shy of Dublin Bottling Works with its giant teal sign looming large over the building, then headed west toward the city park where the town held its Fall Festival. About a block down, he slammed on the brakes. Smack between the Rodeo Heritage Museum and the Lucky Boy Vape shop was a building bearing the name of Dublin Historical Showroom and Guided Audio Tour. He pulled Honey over and went inside through the open doors.

"Greetings," said a girl behind the desk. She was short, with thick black hair and heavy bangs that covered her eyes like the dossan of a highland cow. Sunday placed her in the later teenaged years, probably around twenty or so. Possibly twenty-two, twenty-three.

"Morning," he said. "Uh ..."

"What brings you in?" she asked, bright and friendly. The bangs cleared long enough to for eyes to flash. Big and brown and lined with a paint roller.

"Just, uh, driving through. Got some toilet maintenance in town, but I, uh, saw your place here. Looks interesting." He wanted to ask her if she noticed anything about the sky.

"Oh, it's not my place," said the teen—woman—person. "The city runs it, but my family have always sort of looked after it, kept things up to date." She notched a hand on a hip and gestured to the room's many glass display cases. "Feel free to browse. There's artifacts from the area going back to when we stole the place from the Comanches. And there's a machine over there that will squash a penny and press the town seal into it."

"Alright," said Sunday, wandering to the first case. "Thanks."

"I'm Gabriela if you have any questions. Gabby."

"Sunday."

The display cases contained about what Sunday expected. Accounts of the town's founding (1854), and its founder (A.H. Dobkins), its namesake (a play on the words "Double In" which was the warning cry when the original locals took shelter during Comanche raids). There were write ups on the railroads, local commerce, farming, and it was all exquisitely boring. Sunday sighed as he went along, scanning the history of the town as told by sepia-toned photographs of suited men standing in different places commemorating their grand visions.

He moved to a narrow display case near the back. The theme was the 1936 Erath County Fair. Large, black and white photos showed a massive tent city and all manner of amusements. There were rides, so-called games of skill, old-timey attractions, and oddities like connected twins, miniature families, and the like. There were animals too. Elephants, zebras, horses, posed alongside exotics like a two-headed iguana on a leash and a gazelle with a hoof growing out of its neck. The scale was considerable, even by today's standards. A hand-typed placard leaned against the glass.

ERATH COUNTY FAIR COMES TO DUBLIN

Dublin Mayor Nathan Bryan scored a major coup in 1936 when he forced the uprooting of Erath's annual fair from Stephenville, the county seat, to Dublin for the first time ever. His success was credited to securing the commitment of renowned circus man and traveling carnivalier entertainer-extraordinaire A.V. Cadogan to bring his famed Twilight Faire to Dublin (and indeed to Texas). With Stephenville unable to match the spectacle sure to play out in Dublin, the smaller hamlet secured the bid to hold the fair.

"Now that's a crazy story."

Sunday flinched.

"My bad," said Gabby, clearing her bangs to show an eye. "Didn't mean to frighten you."

"Nah, it's fine. Jumpy lately."

"There's a crazy story about what happened to old Acanthus Cadogan."

"The *carnivalier*?"

"The Shitshow. Ever heard of it?"

Sunday shook his head. "Shitshow?"

Gabby huffed a little chuckle. "That's just what people call it." She tapped the display. "See, this would have put Dublin on the map for good if it had all gone down like it was supposed to. But of course, it didn't." She traced down the glass and pointed to another photo, this one showing a stand full of circus workers and entertainers with an absolute oil derrick of a man standing in the middle foreground with dark goggles and a top hat that practically scraped the clouds. "That's him right there," she said. "That's Cadogan."

Sunday read the caption. *Acanthus Vervain Cadogan Standing Before His Assembled Troupes.* "Hmm. Looks serious."

"Yeah, well, he was. Maybe a little too serious."

"How so?"

"Well, people didn't understand why everything had happened until the workers started talking in the aftermath. Most of them scattered, but there were plenty of accounts that corroborated what went down. Like most circus and carnival barons of the time, it was all about bigger, more, better, faster. Fame and Riches. Chicago World's Fair stuff, you know?"

Sunday didn't. "Hm-mm."

"So, anyway, Cadogan was one of their ilk. He ran his Twilight Faire like a sharecropper. The workers got 'paid' but it went to room and board and expenses. They only fell further into debt even though they worked constantly. But it was more than just the debt or the schedule. His sideshows were famous."

"Bearded ladies and the like?"

"No," said the teen, her voice suddenly grave. "He traded in cruelty. And people came to watch."

"Like ... hurting people?"

"That's the story. Mutilation. Snuff shows."

"Jesus Christ," said Sunday, remembering back to the Faces of Death VHSs his older brother taunted him with in the eighties. He'd been too afraid to watch. "How could the Twilight Faire stay in business if he was doing stuff like that?"

"Sold it as an act. Spectacle. Left enough doubt for people to write it all off as part of the show. But it wasn't."

"How do you know?"

"Well, because the workers finally put an end to it at the Erath County Fair of 1936."

"A carny uprising."

Gabby scowled. "They're called troupers."

"Alright, alright. What did they do?"

She pointed to the next shelf and a picture that to Sunday resembled a giant white teepee against a night sky.

Sunday got down on his knee, grunting as the haunted serpent thing squeezed his calf. Closer in, it was clear that the teepee wasn't a teepee. It was a huge bonfire, overexposed against the black of night. Around its base were the silhouettes of people, putting into scale just how large the fire was.

"They burnt down the fair?"

"Hm-mmm."

"With people in it? Women and kids?"

"No. They set fire to their own quarters first, when that went up, the place cleared out. They burnt down the rest of it after everyone had fled. Everyone but A.V. Cadogan. They had a whole plan for him. The troupers slit the throats of his bodyguards and Pinkertons, then carried him out to the stables. They'd rounded up all the manure, literally tons of shit, into a huge pile. And if you know anything about livestock poop, you know it burns forever."

A subtle nod. "I'm aware."

"So, that's where he went. They tied him up and put him to the torch. It must have taken hours and hours for him to die, just slowly smoldering there. Witnesses said he talked the whole time, like real calm. Saying he'd curse them all. Real specific stuff. He called people by name and told them how they'd die. Said he'd bring the Faire back some day."

"Goddamn."

"Goddamn is right. Anyway, they got tired of him not shutting up and finally just got to shoveling and he cooked alive in a mountain of flaming shit."

"What do you think? You think it's true?"

"What's true?"

Sunday nodded to the display.

"Yeah, it all happened. County Fair never came back to Dublin after that, and here we are. Can't keep anything good. Couldn't hold onto Dr Pepper either."

"I mean, do you believe what Cadogan said?"

"Do I believe his spirit lived on, bent on revenge and planning his return?" She shrugged. "Maybe. All the people who wronged him are probably long dead by now. Still, Dublin has its share of the unexplained."

"I'm in from Glen Rose and there's been some weird stuff happening."

"Like what?"

Like finding a face in a port-a-potty.

Like my mom disappearing through the same one.

Like a stuffed bunny possessed by evil spirits.

"Like, well, have you seen the sky out there?"

"Hmm?"

Sunday walked to the open doors, and out to the street beyond the building's awning. "Come here." He pointed up to the distinctly purple sky.

Gabby peeled away her bangs and shielded her eyes from the sun. "What about it?"

"You don't see the color?"

"Blue?"

"It's not blue, it's fuckin' ... it's purple. Just look at it."

She frowned and looked again. "I don't know, man. Seems the same as always."

He sighed. "Alright. Well, thanks for your help with the, uh, history lesson."

"Sure thing," said Gabby.

"Oh. Where in town was the 1936 County Fair?"

"Just down 6 a little ways. Turn North at the chicken. Dublin City Park."

"Alright, thanks." He made for Honey.

"Hey Sunday?" Gabby reached into her pocket. "Want a free squashed penny with the town seal on it?"

She didn't wait for him to answer and dropped the oblong copper wafer into the big chest pocket on his coveralls. "Thanks."

"Don't spend it all at once." She clicked her tongue and shot a finger gun at him, then went back inside.

Chapter Seven
Visions of the Present Past

B ack in the truck, Sunday's heart pounded. There had to be a connection between the toilet disappearances and A.V. Cadogan's death in flaming elephant dung. Sunday called Gaynes but didn't get an answer. He brought up the tracking app. It showed the geotags less than half a mile away right where Gabriela had told him to go. He went down Highway 6 and turned right at a metal chicken wearing sunglasses, then rolled up to where the sky was darker.

Sunday expected to find a fair or a fall carnival set up, but the park was empty. And *park* was an overstatement. It was an expansive field of mowed grass set beyond a little loop drive. A sad pair of picnic tables hid in a huddle of trees to one side. There was a huge boulder angling up from the grass like a shark's fin, white and sparkling. A piece of limestone maybe? A pond shimmered in the distance. Sitting in the tall grass near the water's edge stood a single yellow porta-potty. It was old, with its southern exposure faded to white. He'd seen those before. Abandoned by whichever company had rented it. They'd probably gone out of business and never picked it up. A damned shame. Happened all the time.

He glanced at his app, then out at the orphaned shitter. He almost didn't want to be right, but there they were: three green dots in a clump two hundred yards away.

He killed the engine and walked out to where the grass began, then glanced back to Honey, and up to the sky. It darkened in an even gradient all the way to an epicenter high above the distant unit. Sunday started across the field, dead and dry as straw, kicking up dust, checking his location against the geotags. They were inside the unit, there was no doubt now, nowhere else they could be. He treaded slowly, the sky darkening with every step. Over his shoulder, Honey sat in a spot of relative sunshine. It was like he'd found the lone cloud on a clear day—like the sky was meant for him, a gathering warning he wasn't heeding.

The sky flashed between light and dark with each step. He halted when it was light. Other than the purple tinted sky, he was in an empty field fifty yards from the old portable. In the next step, he was at the center of the midway hemmed in by ghostly visions of games and wagons full of greasy-sweet food. Another step. It disappeared. But the toilet's door had opened by half. The fair returned with the next footfall, every inch of it wet and dripping, stinking. Another step: daytime Dublin. The next: phantom visions of an olden times fair. At the distant end of the midway, the point of a colossal tent appeared—the big top, its stripes corkscrewing up from the ground like a subterranean drill. In each flash of this dark carnival, it seemed to become real, though there were no people in sight.

"Mom?" he whispered.

He wandered toward an ethereal bottle toss game, the whole world flashing on and off as he went. At the game, he reached out and watched his hand pass through the counter. This place was the answer, there was no doubt now. Blood poured hot through his veins. His mother was here.

Sunday spun toward the big top and started running. The world flickered around him like film drawn through a projector. In half the cells, the portable came closer, its door widening. In the other half, it was the tent twisting up from the earth. He slowed near the entrance, as all the world swapped light and dark, *tik tik tik*, until he stood before the big canvas flap.

The Ringmaster's grand voice boomed from inside the tent, see-sawing over the crowd and calling their attention to the amusements they were soon to witness. "Come and see the Lobster Boy! Turn your eyes to the Scribe of Hades but don't let him see you blink! Who has the stomach to have your organs tickled by Erasmus, the blind swordsman? Who here came seeking thrills? Who here came to find excitement? Who came to ..." Then the voice became syrupy, drawn out like a record slowing down. It sped up again and the voice changed, higher pitched and lighter, saying, "Who came ... *to find what was lost?*"

"Mom?" Breathless, Sunday lurched for the tent flap.

His balance was off. He was falling, falling, until the ground stopped him. Everything was bright and yellow. And stank. The fair was gone. Somehow, he'd thrown himself through the door of the portable, knocked it over, and was now prone against the inside wall. He crawfished away from the tank as dribble of ancient sludge wormed from the hole and slid over the lid. The unmistakable impressions of three geotags lumped the soupy mix. The unit started to rumble. He scooted away and stood up out of the door, which opened to the purple-tainted daytime sky.

Sunday pulled himself out of the door hole using his belly to hold him in place as he caught his breath. His weight shifted the balance and the unit rolled to the side, throwing him headfirst into the grass with an indecorous grunt. The leg parasite was tighter and hotter, like being inside the ghost fair had excited it. He scrambled up and tried standing the unit back up, but it vibrated with a hostile energy.

"Fuck it," he said, and ran stumbling toward Honey.

He pulled out his phone to call Ms. Poppy, but let it slip into the dust. Hands shaking like the leaves on a burr oak, he fumbled for it, then couldn't even enter the password to make a call. Life had prepared him for a lot of things—*well, no: his mother* had prepared him, and that by herself. But this? Whatever this was went beyond parental advice. Helplessness wasn't a label he'd ever self-applied, but it was a brutal truth right now. His mother was lost, at her most vulnerable, and he couldn't stop panicking long enough to punch the right buttons on his phone.

"Get your shit together, Sunday."

He held his breath, squeezed his hands, flexed his fingers, then slowly tapped the contact for Ms. Poppy.

"Hel—"

"Ms. Poppy!"

"Sunday? You okay?"

"Thank God you're fine. Stay away from ..." He tripped and nearly fell over. "... stay away from that fucking portable Ms. Poppy! And if anyone goes near it—if those Doucet kids get close—"

"Already chased the little dildos off twice. Used my bb gun. Hit the girl, I think. One of 'em's a girl, right?"

"You can't shoot kids, Ms. Poppy!"

"They're trash goblins!"

"Anyhow, don't do anything else and don't go near that portable!" He jumped into Honey's cab. "I know where Mom is! I'll be there in forty-five."

"That's great! Get me a case of that Dublin Red Cola, will you?"

"No time!" He ended the call and tossed the phone out the passenger side window. "Goddamit!"

Honey shot down the Highway at near eighty, which was twenty past the speed she wanted to go, and Sunday hoped she'd hold together back to Glen Rose.

The phone rang.

"Gaynes?"

"Yeah, uh, hi there," said the Donut Shark. "Just checking in with you. Sorry, still haven't seen any sign of Regina."

"Yeah, I know."

"What? What do you mean *you know*?"

What was he going to do? Tell the cops she'd been swept into a dark carnival realm through a rental toilet? "Nothing, just ... it's been two days? It's Glen Rose. Where could she be?"

"Is there something you're not telling me?"

Yes. "No."

There was a pause on the other side. Sunday realized Gaynes was now considering he might have played a part in his mother's disappearance.

He had to nip that in the bud. "I didn't do anything to my own mother, Gaynes. I've been taking care of her every day for two years since she moved in. I've given up everything for her."

"Hm-mm."

"Wait a second, you're not seriously considering me ... you're not..."

"Listen here: this is not the time to hold back on me. Am I a small-time cop? Yeah, now maybe. But I did twelve years with the sheriff up in Wichita Falls." It sounded like *Wichitawl Fawls* the way he said it. "I know when someone's engaging in an act of omission. Where are you anyways?"

"I'm uh—Dublin."

"Sure you're not on your way back from Goldthwaite?"

Sunday's heart jumped a little. "Goldthwaite? Why would I be there?"

"Okay, okay. Tell me why you're in Dublin."

"Neighbor wanted some of that 1891 Red Soda."

"Oh yeah? Mom goes missing and you traipse over to Dublin for black market Dr. Pepper?"

"Well, they were out."

"I think we should talk, face to face."

"I'm pretty busy."

"You got time for Red Soda; you got time for me. Come by the station at 6:00 p.m."

"You want to ask me something right now, go ahead and ask."

"Six p.m. Don't make me come get you."

The line went dead.

The Donut Shark had picked up the scent of his deception, only it didn't carry the stink of matricide he thought it did. Nevertheless, the deputy was circling Sunday as if he were a wounded blueberry cruller.

This presented a new aspect to Sunday's dilemma. Because even though the deputy was a Grade A Dipshit, he carried the force of law.

Chapter Eight

Spelunking

Ms. Poppy was doing her best Wyatt Earp, leaning over the handrail of her steps having a smoke while surveilling Live Oaks Enclave like it was main street in Tombstone. A bb gun rifle remained within reach, leaned against her trailer. She hollered as Sunday came around Honey's front. "The Doucets have cleared out for now. I don't think we'll be seeing much more—"

"They got another report, Ms. Poppy. Down in Goldthwaite. Just came in. They think I'm involved somehow, or at least that I had something to do with Mom."

Ms. Poppy puffed on her cigar. "Well, they do say it's family members ninety-five percent of the time."

"I don't think it's that high. Hey! Obviously, it's not me." Sunday's heart was pounding in his ear like Lemmy's bass. His vision pulsed red. "I gotta ... I gotta think."

He swiped a rope of sweat from his brow. Goddamned autumn in Texas.

Hissing from the pain in his calf, he limped up the steps to his trailer and checked his watch. Three-thirty p.m. For all that happened on the day it should have been later, but he was glad it wasn't. He had two and a half hours until his date with the Donut Shark. Sitting gingerly on the kitchenette bench, he pulled off his coveralls and his left boot, then went to work on the right, where the bunny remnant had become one with the leather. He picked at it, wincing with every touch, guessing that it wasn't ever coming off. Not unless he could put an end to whatever in the cursed hell was going on. Fearing sepsis, he found a bottle of rubbing alcohol and drenched the wound to disinfect the area. It only quadrupled his pain, and he yowled like a cat in a bathtub.

He threw on some shorts and an old Motörhead concert tee, sat down at the table in the kitchenette, and tried to take account of what he'd learned and what he thought he knew.

His mother, Regina McWhorter, was trapped in a spectral dimension. No doubt summoned into a spirit world of dark carnivals by the shit-tainted ghost of A.V. Cadogan. No wonder he'd chosen portable sewage containers as his path back into the world. They were numerous, everywhere, and contained the medium with which his body and spirit had become entwined.

He ran outside, ripped open the door to the portable and jumped in. "Come on! Show yourself you son-bitch!" He shouted into the tank. "Give me my mother back! Take me instead! I'm right here! Come and face me!" He kicked the tank over and over, then stumbled outside.

"Sunday?" said Ms. Poppy, her voice soft. She preferred not to walk but had ambled down from her perch. "You gotta stop that. You're going to hurt yourself."

"Why won't it take me, Ms. Poppy? It took Mom. Why won't it take me?"

She pressed in and wrapped her arms around him. Standing nearly two feet taller than the tiny woman, he returned the embrace.

"I have a crazy idea. I just need you to hear it out, alright?"

"Sure, whatever you need."

"Come here." He led her into his trailer and to the map spread over the kitchenette table. "See, here's the places where people have disappeared. And they all point to Dublin. I dropped some geo tags, these little trackers, into different portables. Here and Stephenville. They ended up in this abandoned toilet unit in Dublin. And see, Dublin was the location of this terrible catastrophe in 1936 involving this bad old carnival boss. Acanthus Vervain Cadogan. His ghost is coming back somehow. Trying to manifest his Twilight Faire into the real world."

"I had a cousin try that once. Down in Shreveport."

"Huh?"

"Not the carnival boss bit. Jerry was a gold dealer. Got killed by his partner. Came back from the dead. Partner was found tied to an anchor in Cross Lake."

Sunday had a number of follow-up questions but saved them for future conversation. "Sure. Well, look, there's all these places where people have gone missing. Glen Rose, Proctor, Stephenville, Valera, Clifton, Waco, Cisco, Anson. Oh, and," he said, then picked up a pen and circled the new city, "Goldthwaite." He considered the map, then took up the ruler, drawing a line from Goldthwaite through Dublin and kept going until it intersected another town.

"Mineral Wells."

"What about it?"

"The disappearances come in pairs. The next person is going to come from Mineral Wells. That's Palo Pinto County, right? Do they have a fair?"

"Mineral Wells is too big for me. I don't know."

Sunday did a web search.

"There's one of those traveling carnival things at the Mineral Wells Eastside Convention parking lot." He looked at Ms. Polly, wild-eyed. "I gotta go!"

"What are you going to do?"

He shot out the door, hollering back, "Get abducted!"

"You gotta get that leg checked out. You smell like a burnt asshole."

Sunday jumped into Honey and took her around the loop to the doublewide trailer of Calvin Teague, Esquire. He ran up and pounded on the door. Calvin Teague was a person Sunday thought of as a modern-day pioneer. The man had done it all. He'd been an oil man, a lawyer, a dentist, biographer to the lesser-known, and deep-sea fisherman-slash-coral reef explorer. Nowadays, though, he was a shut-in who spent most of his time exploring the limits of his own inebriation.

The door swung open with Teague standing there in an apron emblazoned with the picture of a dinosaur in a Corvette, crotch hugging jorts, and boat shoes.

"Sunday McWhorter! I was about to throw a sirloin in the oven. You want one? They come frozen."

"I can't right now, Mr. Teague. I'm sorry. I've got a big problem and you're the only one who can h—"

"The Doucets?"

"No. Um. Look, do you still have any of your scuba gear?"

"You going diving?" Teague looked him over. "I didn't put you for a diver."

"First time. Just need to borrow the gear."

"Say no more. Rental fees are downright usurious these days. Of course, I don't know how my stuff would fit on you. You're big enough to stick in a cornfield."

"I'm fine with a tight fit."

"That's what you're gonna get. Alright. Let me find my keys."

Teague disappeared momentarily, then came out and led Sunday to the side of his home, where an old sunfish sailboat sat atop a trailer with flat tires. He unlocked a storage compartment revealing a musty pile of black rubber and plastic. The old man pulled it out and piled it in Sunday's arms.

"Can't promise it's still watertight. Should probably get you to sign a release." He locked eyes with Sunday. "Just kiddin' son, you can sue me if you want, but you know, blood from a stone and all that."

Sunday shook his head.

"Hey," said Teague, setting an oval facemask atop the gear. "Did you find your mother? Wait a minute. Oh no, do they think she's in a lake? That what this is about?"

"No, Mr. Teague. This is for something else."

"That's fine. You don't have to tell me. Hey, this rebreather is shot! You might have to rent that. I got a snorkel if you want."

Sunday nodded.

"Still don't think this stuff will fit. But hey, if it rips, just throw it away for me, a'right?"

"Sure, thanks Mr. Teague."

"Calvin."

"Okay."

He put the gear in the cab and drove off. He had to make Mineral Wells before the carnival opened and smuggle himself into Cadogan's Twilight Faire before he officially became a wanted man.

Sunday found the carnival setup right where the Internet said it would be, spread across the parking lot of a sorry looking convention arena. He circled the temporary fencing around the perimeter. Traveling carnivals were a special breed of entertainment, one that prior to recent events Sunday had enjoyed, as a younger man at least. They were fun and colorful, but more than that, they were seedy and dangerous, a perfect combination for a night out with friends. There was a time that Sunday and his crew slammed cheap beer and rode the Himalaya (or an even cheaper copy of the Himalaya) until one of them barfed.

The place was empty and would be until dark. He had an hour. A kid with a stringy ZZ Top beard let him drive right in as not a lot of people were running clandestine operations from a honeywagon. Twenty portables lined the back corner of the lot. He hopped out and secured nineteen doors with zip-ties, then pulled the scuba gear from the cab. It was dusty and stuck together in places. He practically ground his teeth into caliche trying to pull the legs apart. Panting for air, he realized he hadn't thought this through. He was exposed. Of course, if he tried changing inside the unit, he might get sucked to shit city in his undies. He quickly disrobed down to his tighty-whities and packed himself into the wetsuit, wrenching the zipper up over his belly. The hood was too tight, forcing him to retreat the zipper a few inches so the collar didn't choke him out.

He looked like a fool. The sleeves didn't even reach his wrists. The pants barely covered his calves. The tail end of the demon eel peeked out from the cuff. He considered the diving boots. There was no way they'd fit. He leaned over and yanked his work boots back on, grunting as the wetsuit constricted his diaphragm. It was starting to get dark.

The teen with the beard came walking down the fence line. He called over. "We're gonna open soon. Can you get that truck moved?"

Sunday hollered back, "Sorry kid, these units are all out of order!"

The kid's eyes ballooned. "All of 'em? What are we supposed to do?"

"Leave me alone so I can get them fixed."

He seemed to see Sunday's getup for the first time. "Looks serious."

"Yeah, you could say that." Sunday gestured to the open portable. "Do you mind if I do my job now?"

"What's the matter with them?"

"Plumbing's fucked."

"They have plumbing?"

Sunday shook his head. "There's a good deal about the portable latrine you probably don't know. I got work to do."

The teen hustled off, probably to give the bad news to his superiors. Sunday was running out of time. He went to the toilet and was about to step in, when a notion struck him. The place he'd seen in the vision in Dublin City Park didn't look so friendly. He should have a weapon. Some form of self-defense, at least. He stomped over and punched open Honey's glove compartment. Inside was a Swiss Army knife no larger than his pinky and a glass-break hammer with a small seatbelt knife in case he ever put Honey into Lake Granbury. He grabbed both and jumped into the porta-potty, shut the door and locked it. Then waited.

Obviously, there hadn't been any abductions yet from Mineral Wells. This had to be the way to get to the other side, to the Twilight Faire or whatever it was. He waited, sweating the scuba suit into a walking swamp. In only minutes it had become unbearable. A skintight bog.

Nothing was happening. He jumped out and ran to the truck for his phone and a handful of geotags, then back into the unit. He tossed one of the tags into the tank and brought up his phone. It just sat there. Glancing outside, he saw the bearded teen returning with a larger group. Sunday locked himself inside.

Knocking.

"Occupied!" said Sunday, slipping his phone into a plastic baggie on account of the sewage.

"Hey, in there!" yelled a man. "Ezekiel says you decommissioned the toilets."

"Yeah," echoed Sunday from inside. "Sorry about that."

"Well, why? What's the matter with them? Someone was by earlier today and did all the routine maintenance already. He didn't say anything."

There was no honest explanation. Portables were a tank with toilet hole built into a phone booth. He answered with, "Protocol. Regulations."

"What's that supposed to mean? We're opening up right now. People are coming in. Where are they supposed to do their business?"

"I'm working on that," said Sunday, getting sweatier by the second. Why wasn't he being teleported to Dublin?

"Sorry, did you say you're working on it?"

"Yeah."

"Why's the door shut?"

"Cause y'all keep distracting me."

More knocking. Louder. Angrier.

"Alright, come out of there."

The door rumbled as they tried to open it.

"Stop that!" yelled Sunday. "Call Central Texas Temporary Sanitation if you want to file a complaint." Sunday checked his phone. The geotag was sliding slowly south by southwest towards Dublin. *Holy shit.*

His ankle went hot as a bed of coals. He stifled a cry.

The portable rumbled as outside the carnival workers—were these just regular workers or *troupers* as Gabby had called them?—pushed on the sides. Sunday shoved the phone into a chest pocket and braced himself between the walls. Tank water sloshed side to side and splashed out of the hole, and it was at this moment that Sunday remembered that wetsuits are not indeed waterproof but rather designed to keep one warm in a frigid aqueous environment. He wasn't cold and water was only a component of what he'd face in a toilet spelunking situation.

He pressed against the wall.

Even with the sound of the portable being knocked back and forth, Sunday heard something else. A deep, ominous rumbling from the tank. The sound of splashing suddenly broadened, echoing below as if he stood upon the roof of a great cavern over a subterranean lake. And something lurked in its waters. It gurgled, then hissed, air rasping through a serpentine throat. The carnival lights outside illuminated the plastic walls like a Chinese lantern, and the silhouette of a thick, vein-covered stalk emerged from the hole.

"What's going on in there?"

The stalk split open like a squash blossom and spread its petals.

Chapter Nine
Portal Potty

I t wasn't Sunday's life that flashed before his eyes, but his mother's life through his. Every memory of her since childhood. Being pulled in a wagon with his favorite green bear, watching her hand paint children's show characters on poster board and hang them on the walls so their tiny home would have some color, letting him drink coffee in middle school because that's what you did when you were the man of the house.

He remembered them moving a lot, his mother turning to him with an easy smile whenever it got hard, telling him that she would always take care of him no matter what, and him telling her that no, he would take care of her.

And now he'd broken his promise.

Sunday supposed he'd expected to be eaten by the giant meat flower but soon realized that wasn't his destiny.

The stalk reached the ceiling of the unit, curved over and opened wider, spreading down the walls. Fleshy tendrils lashed out from its expanding throat, catching Sunday on the arm and leg with razor talons slashing through both wetsuit and skin. Sunday's mind was elsewhere, focused upon the image of the blue-stained face of the teen Roy West Carpenter, and he quickly yanked down the diving mask and covered the bottom of his face with his hands, then sank to the floor and pulled his knees in tight. The spiral of bunny carcass glowed like orange neon in his flesh.

The inside of the unit was quickly covered in spiked membrane borne of the toilet hole and things began to quaver and shift. The walls expanded and contracted, a trick of the mind, surely. Sunday reached out to touch the plastic tank and felt it pulling and moving as easy as putty. Rings of light reminiscent of oil rainbows in a puddle pulsed along the length of the stalk and then down the walls where its skin had spread. Holes appeared in this new flesh, each wide enough to pass an egg. A blackened purple slurry dribbled from these orifices and Sunday shriveled away. The smell made him think of the time he found a dead racoon under the kitchen sink as a child. He tried to breathe from his mouth, but the stench was thick enough to taste. Such was his disgust, he almost forgot to be afraid.

And then he remembered.

Sunday screeched as the walls collapsed inward, trapping him inside like vacuum sealed deer jerky.

A brief sensation of momentum and freezing cold. The strange organ unraveled from around him, folded into itself, and disappeared down the hole. *A new hole.* Not the one from the portable he'd walked into. This hole was cut into a wooden box inside a wooden closet—no, an outhouse, an arcane latrine from centuries of yore. Sunday's legs wobbled as he stood, coated in some sort of meat jelly like what protects a Vienna sausage from spoiling, except purpler. Trying to scrape it off his face and body, he stumbled and fell through the rickety wooden door behind him onto the muddy ground.

The plum-black sky loomed overhead. Somewhere music played, a once cheery melody on old strings, out of time and tune. An organ grinder moaned somewhere out of view, playing too fast, then too slow. Sunday pushed to his feet.

The outhouse was just like in westerns, all janky and planked together with rough-cut lumber. It had two giant wagon wheels affixed to the sides, allowing someone to lean it back and roll it around.

A truly portable potty.

He turned slowly, feeling strangely familiar with the place and not just because he'd seen snippets in visions. It was the air, the stars, not something he could quite put his finger on. In the distance, a rock thrust out from the mud like the bleached white tooth of some long dead behemoth. Yes, he had been here before. It was Dublin City Park. Only, different. A parallel dimension like they say.

Cadogan's Twilight Faire spread across the land, raised from the ashes. Before, in the vision, everything had been a blur, but now Sunday was here. There were food carts and games, all wood and canvas, set against a backdrop of tents containing every amusement imaginable.

Big, hand-painted letters on boards nailed high over the nearest attraction announced it as the *Devil's Whip*. There were cars set around a loop, attached to a central hub by rope. Sunday could see it play out, the cars going around and literally whipping through the turns. Presently, it stood unmoving, without riders or an operator. He wandered down the line, past the *Mournful-Go-Round*, the *Chair-O-Plane*, *Doom Bingo*, the *Eurasian Freak Maze*, a familiar looking ride called the *Tilt-N-Hurl*, as well as others that were entirely foreign to his eyes: the *Knife Dodge*, *Gut Scrambler*, and the *Perpetual Wheel*. This last ride was like a Ferris Wheel, only with a second wheel inside the first, set perpendicularly. It made him nauseous. He gazed down the length of the midway, expecting to see the crown jewel of any circus, but it wasn't there. The terrible spinning big top tent from his visions was missing. The midway simply ended at an expanse of mud and straw.

A glint of light caught Sunday's attention, and he crossed the midway to an attraction on the opposite side. The sign dubbed it *The Skinner*. There was a central, vase-shaped piece about thirty feet tall. Long, curving arms sprouted from the body and curved gracefully up the vase to meet at the top. Each arm dipped slightly out at the tips, high up over the Faire, and attached to the end of each was a capsule for the rider.

Sunday tracked a wet noise, like someone coughing up phlegm, to a single capsule gently swaying on its hinges. A doleful moan came from inside and the arm began to descend. As it did, Sunday understood the workings of the ride better. It was less a vase and more an octopus-like construction, with eight arms, each grasping one of the riding compartments like a bauble. Sunday had always appreciated octopuses for their intelligence.

The arm reached the ground, and the capsule swung side to side as its occupant shifted. The capsule was made of the same steel lattice design of most amusement rides, but this one was different up close. Each of the diamond-shaped openings was raised on one end and depressed on the other. Holes that if a body were to rub the wrong way, would slice the skin like a cheese grater.

"You workin' or playin'?" It was a young man's voice, clear as day, that rang out from inside the pod. "If it's playin' you're early. If it's workin', you're right on time."

He coughed again and gagged. The capsule opened. A booted foot connected to a denim-bound leg stomped the mud and a pair of eyes gleamed out from the shadows. A man emerged from the ride, lanky and faceless.

Sunday knew immediately. "Roy Carpenter?"

The teen paused. "How do you know who I am?" The "m" sound came out as a sharper "n" sound on account of his having no lips.

Sunday stepped close and looked around to see if they were being observed. It felt like they were. "I'm Sunday McWhorter, sanitary technician. I, uh, I think I recovered your face from a toilet in Glen Rose."

Roy was hard to read without the assistance of expressions, though his lidless eyes suggested astonishment. He reached slowly up and touched the raw meat of his cheek, as if he'd forgotten his face had been shorn. His arms and hands were pocked with tiny divots where the skin had been scooped to the quick by the cheese grater ride.

Sunday approached another step, but the teen balked.

"I just want to know what's going on here. What is this place?"

Roy glanced back at *The Skinner*. "The Twilight Faire?"

"Yeah."

"We operate it."

"Who's we?"

"Troupers like me and you.

"Nah, no," said Sunday, waving his hand. "I'm not here to work. I need to find my mom. Regina McWhorter. Have you seen her?"

Roy stared as it was the only way for him to regard anyone.

"Roy? You see my mom?"

"That way." Roy pointed in the direction of the old toilet, still sitting in the center of the midway. "Or could be that way," he said, gesturing in the opposite direction.

"You don't know."

"I operate *The Skinner*."

Sunday put it together. "Can you not leave?"

Roy panned the midway, then set his huge eyes on Sunday. "I operate *The Skinner*."

"Okay, but you have to tell me what's going on. Where is everyone else? Where's Cadogan?"

"Shhhhh," said Roy, placing a flayed index finger over his exposed teeth and gums. The raw flesh of his brow furrowed like skirt steak. "You're an operator like us. When you find your amusement, you'll know. And you'll serve." He stomped back to the capsule hanging from the end of its metal tentacle.

"Roy!"

The teen was already crawling inside. The door closed and the latch clicked. Then the entire machine slowly spun, and as it did, the arm ascended until it met with the others at the top. The capsule squeaked a few times and went still.

Sunday stepped back into the midway. He checked the latrine as if it was a getaway car. As far as he knew, it was the only way out, if it even worked in reverse. He walked down the line of attractions, past the *Tumble-Bones*, the *Human Fly*, *Hot Scotch*, *Chokelahoma*, and even a sideshow tent with INFLAMMABLE CHILD lettered on the awning. Assuming the troupers and ride operators to be hibernating somewhere inside, Sunday scurried past in search of the one specific attraction he figured might bear fruit.

Something ambled stiffly from the shadows as he neared the end of the midway. It came into the light, a young woman carrying a serving platter. Entrails dangled from a hole in her belly over the front of a short skirt. Fortunately, she retained her face. But her eyes were milky, with the mild impression of irises barely visible beneath a nacreous film. She opened her mouth and croaked like a zombie from video games. A few words gurgled out. "Got ... funnel cake?"

Sunday smelled it. The greasy aroma of fried batter. He'd never liked it in the corporeal world, and it was far worse in the Twilight Faire. Rancid. Sour. It burnt his nostrils something vicious. He lowered his head and tried to walk by, but the woman shuffled in front of him.

"I run that floss wagon," she said, pointing to a janky cart on wheels with a setup for boiling oil. "S'good. See?"

She grabbed a wad of the offal-shaped pastry tubes in her filthy fingers and lifted it dripping into her misshapen mouth, smacking like a lizard swallowing an insect. A wet, slapping noise drew Sunday's eyes to the ground, where the masticated dough fell in lumps below her gaping ribcage and shredded organs.

She smiled sympathetically at Sunday's shock, saying only, "I won't die."

It could have been a statement of reassurance. But that wasn't how he heard it. What he heard was lamentation. She wanted to die, she just couldn't.

"I'm looking for my mother. Her name is Regina McWhorter."

"Regina McWhorter," she repeated flatly. "Regina McWhorter."

"Yes. Do you know—"

"Regina McWhorter."

Sunday peeled himself away, giving the disemboweled teen a wide berth. She followed for a bit, offering more swampy donut noodles, but halted like a dog on a rope when she got to a point. Like Roy Carpenter, she seemed tethered to her station.

Up ahead, a second thoroughfare intersected the midway like the horizontal bar of a crucifix. All the way down to the left he found what he was looking for. The last attraction in line.

Chapter Ten

Un-house

The "F" wasn't missing. The hand-lettered sign was clear: *UN-HOUSE*. Sunday didn't like the feeling it put off, like standing beside a black hole and just waiting for it to his suck his identity down its throat and be lost forever. But it was clearly the Faire's version of a funhouse and that meant it was where he'd find his mom if she had any choice at all about where to be found.

The food wagon to the right of the *Un-house* reeked of boiling hot-dogs even though the sign hanging on front read *Candied Apples*. The silhouette of someone sitting in a chair shifted within the shadows of a pop-up tent behind it. Sunday considered making another inquiry, but so far it seemed none of the Faire workers were keen on the world beyond their stations. And selfishly, he didn't care to see the state of the person currently veiled by darkness.

He went to the foot of the *Un-house* stairs and gazed into the darkened entrance. For a flash he saw it as the portable unit stored back home, door wide open, his mother standing inside urging him to join her. It wasn't a pleasant thought. Even normal funhouses weren't Sunday's thing, but they'd always gone through them together and come out unscathed. But now, if she was inside, he feared what might have become of her. What if she was in some mangled state, all joints bent the wrong way and her head on backwards? He didn't want to think about that, but it didn't mean he wasn't going to have to. And soon. He took the first step.

The entrance was a short, dark passage leading to a set of large wooden doors painted with the warped face of a laughing clown. Sunday paused, one hand ready to push them open, then backed away to better see the image as his eyes adjusted. It wasn't a clown at all, but a man. A bright red face with brighter red eyes and a thin, curling mustache drawn in black above a wide yellow grin. Cadogan?

Sunday registered a spike of fear. His instincts were tripping faults, telling him in no uncertain terms DO NOT PROCEED. The Faire was plenty scary, but the *Un-house* stood waiting, like an unopened box not filled with anything good. Even if she was inside, Sunday expected the worst. And what was that, anyway? Those horrors your mind can't even conceive of, the unknown: that's what really made his spine tingle. But if his mom was in there, she'd already confronted her fear and swallowed it down. And that was the only reason he palmed the door and went inside.

Faintly flickering candelabras cast tepid light along the walls of a narrow hall. Framed photographs displayed blurry scenes of anonymous people in awkward, pseudo-sexual poses. A man hung suspended in a web of rope like spider bait. One shot was taken through the thick porthole of a furnace, with children sitting inside. A woman stood at a cliff's precipice overlooking a void. Sunday felt witness to the moment she decided to let herself fall. He told himself that this world wasn't real, that these pictures didn't really exist. None of the suffering they showed had ever been experienced.

It didn't help.

The hallway ended at another door he recognized because it was the door to his singlewide back in Glen Rose. Only, he wasn't in Glen Rose. He went in.

A plate sat on the kitchenette table smeared in egg yolk and Cholula sauce. Someone had just finished eating. Feeling a bit like Goldilocks, he picked up the bottle and wiggled it. Felt real. He continued toward the far end and rapped on the door to his mother's room.

"Mom?"

He opened it only to be confronted by an image of *himself*.

He'd always hated the hall of mirrors, especially now since it reminded him how he was dressed. He looked like he'd stolen a child's scuba suit and packed himself inside. The cuffs pulled up on his forearms and calves, and his stomach ballooned the middle like runaway biscuit dough. He powered ahead and watched himself multiply to infinity.

Disorientation came fast. The light was dim and amber. The mirrors went from merely everywhere to bending and twisting. The massive forehead and tiny beard of his own distorted face was everywhere.

"Mom?"

A blemish on a mirror caught his eye, words scrawled in greasy black.

Is that you, Regina McWhorter?

He touched it, smearing his mother's name, then felt his way along the glass until his fingers found an edge. Another turn of the maze.

There, handwriting filled every inch of mirror from ceiling to floor. The writing was small, like in a secret diary, written to the edges and with little room left between the lines. He leaned in and tilted his head.

You were born Regina Christine Jacobs to Alaster and Nancy Jacobs on a sweltering August

MORNING. YOU WERE A LIVELY AND PRECOCIOUS CHILD. IN SCHOOL, YOU SHOWED AN AFFINITY FOR SINGING AND THE-ATER, BEGINNING AT SEVEN YEARS OLD IN YOUR SCHOOL'S PRODUCTION OF WHAT I WANT FOR CHRISTMAS, AND SENDING THE AUDIENCE INTO AN UPROAR WITH YOUR OFF-SCRIPT NON-SEQUITURS. YOUR FAMILY WAS POOR, YOU GREW UP TOO SOON.

Sunday swallowed hard as he moved along. Why was he reading the story of his mother's life?

AT AGE NINETEEN, YOU FELL IN LOVE. HE WAS TEN YEARS OLDER, BUT HE WAS A WAY OUT OF A LIFE THAT WAS GOING NOWHERE. HE MADE PROMISES AND YOU BELIEVED THEM. THERE WERE THINGS ABOUT HIM, GOOD THINGS THAT REMINDED YOU OF YOUR FATHER. BLUE EYES LIKE THE HORIZON AT DUSK, THE ABILITY TO MAKE A STRANGER LAUGH UNTIL THEIR CHEEKS ACHED. IT WASN'T LONG BE-FORE YOU LEARNED THAT HE WAS LIKE YOUR FATHER IN OTHER WAYS TOO. A TEMPER LIKE FIREWORKS, FISTS AS HEAVY AS IRON.

His mother had never told him any of this. Was it true? So much made sense now—like why she never let him see his grandparents. Why she never talked about them other than in vagaries that made them sound fictional.

YOU HAD ONE CHILD, A SON YOU NAMED AFTER THE WEATHER ON THE DAY HE WAS BORN. SUN-DAY. THIS BOY BECAME YOUR PURPOSE. YOU VOWED HE WOULD NOT SUFFER A CHILDHOOD OF PARALYZING FEAR AS YOU HAD.

SO, WHEN THE TIME WAS RIGHT, YOU BUNDLED HIM TIGHT AND FLED FOREVER.

The words blurred as tears pooled on his eyes. And not because it shattered the lie she'd told him of a wonderful father who died when Sunday was too young to remember. His face went hot with rage at this man he'd never known, and he cried that he couldn't go back in time and stop him.

He ran through the maze of grease paint memories, recklessly so, bouncing through twists and turns. He pulled up short before crashing face first into a new wall of words.

YOU REALIZED YOU WERE STARTING TO FORGET. AND IT WAS THE MOST IMPORTANT THINGS YOU WERE FORGETTING. YOU HAD ALWAYS BEEN FIERCELY INDEPENDENT. YOU LOST YOUR HOUSE AND MOVED AWAY FROM FRIENDS TO A NEW PLACE. THIS WAS THE PLACE YOU WOULD LIVE UNTIL YOU DIED FROM THE ROT IN YOUR MIND. THE DAYS BLURRED TOGETHER AND SOON THEY WERE EXACTLY THE SAME. SOME MORNINGS A MAN WITH A BEARD SERVED YOU EGGS. OFTEN YOU HAD NO APPETITE BUT YOU ATE THEM BECAUSE HE TOLD YOU TO AND YOU WERE SCARED WHAT WOULD HAPPEN IF YOU REFUSED. THE MORNINGS WERE THE WORST, AND YOU WOKE GRIPPED BY FEAR.

Sunday rubbed his eyes and face, realizing why his mother sometimes froze up when he embraced her in the kitchenette. Why her plate was always cleaned. She must have thought he was his father.

He pressed farther into the labyrinth.

With one hand grazing the glass off his shoulder and another out in front, Sunday made slow progress. When the path forked, he chose a way without stopping to think about it or read more of the biographical scratch.

Something scurried in the corner of his eye. Turning his head, he looked to where the main passageway took off in a zigzag, and the reflections seemed to build on each other like a tessellation. It made him dizzy. Somewhere distant, yet reflected to a place mere feet away, a corner of glass where a new hallway began.

She was there, hunched on the floor, stringy black hair spread across the naked skin of her orange-painted shoulders. She moved furtively, like a rat shaving wood for its nest, intent on her writing. The convex surface of the mirror's undulation made her look small, like a strange crustacean.

"Mom?"

"I'm writing it all down, baby. There's so much. My whole life. No one can take it away if it's written down. Have to get it all down."

Sunday stepped to where he thought the passage went, only to bump another mirror.

"I write and I write. You have no idea the sensation of remembering after losing so much. It's like being pulled from the water before drowning. I'm breathing again. Come and see, come and see."

He tried another direction but went backward and was lost again. His mother was out of view but he could still hear her.

"Tell me how to get to you."

"Just follow the story. It's my life. All of it."

"I saw."

"Whatever you have lost, you will find it here."

"I lost you, Mom," he offered, feeling around a corner.

"And you have found me in exactly the place I need to be," she answered brightly. "It's thanks to you. You showed me the way. You presented a door. I only walked forward. You're the best son a mother could ever ask for."

He followed the sound of her voice, trying to get closer. One way and her voice would go faint. Another direction, and she seemed just around the corner. He read bits of the text as he went. "Why do you write it like this?"

YOU OFTEN WOKE DURING THE NIGHT TO FIND THE SHEETS SOAKED WITH SWEAT AND FEARFUL FOR YOURSELF AND YOUR SON. OFTEN, YOU SHOVED CLOTHES INTO A BAG AND PREPARED TO RUN INTO HIS ROOM SO YOU MIGHT SPIRIT HIM AWAY BEFORE YOUR ABSENCE WAS DISCOVERED, ONLY TO REALIZE THAT YOUR SON WAS A GROWN MAN AND THAT YOU NO LONGER HAD REASON TO RUN. YOU WENT TO BED EVERY NIGHT KNOWING THERE WAS A CHANCE YOU'D WAKE UP AGAIN, NOT REMEMBERING WHAT YEAR IT WAS, HEART POUNDING, CONVINCED THAT ESCAPE WAS THE ONLY WAY YOU'D SURVIVE. AS YOUR MIND SHED ITS LAYERS, IT ONLY GOT WORSE.

"I didn't know," he whispered. Then he called to her, "I didn't know you were so afraid. I didn't know that you thought I was him sometimes."

"I prefer to remember, baby, even if some of the memories are painful."

"Why are you writing it like this? Like you're writing the story of your life, but as a character in it."

"Oh, I'm writing exactly what I hear. Exactly as it is told to me."

Sunday stopped. "Somebody is telling you the story of your life?"

"Filling in all the blanks. Giving me back what I'd lost. A Good Samaritan. Helping me."

Sunday ran, crashing into walls, slamming his face into panes of glass with no mirror behind them at all. His nose cracked. "Mom!" He raced through the maze. "Mom! Where are you?" He blasted around a corner. And then he found her.

Regina McWhorter stood on the ceiling at the distant end of a long corridor, cast red, grinning wide and yellow. "I'm right here."

Chapter Eleven

Urchins

"You're on the ceiling, Mom."

"The mirrors must have turned me around."

He ran down the corridor only to slam into another pane of glass dividing the hallway in two. His mother walked toward him. Her path spiraled from the ceiling to the wall, and finally to the floor, and he thought maybe it was a trick of the place that made her seem like a ceiling walker. Her skin stayed unclothed and bright orange, her fingers stained black from whatever ink she used to craft her memoir. Soon they were face to face. Another pane of glass stopped him when he reached out to touch her.

"How do we get out?" asked Sunday.

She looked around as if for a clue to the answer. "I don't ... I don't know. I've never wanted to leave. I'm not allergic to the crawfish here." Her voice came garbled and distant, as if she was submerged in a creek.

"Mom. Listen to me. This is not—this is fucked. Where are your clothes?"

She shrugged.

"I'm going to try some other ways to get to you. Stay right—what?"

She'd put a finger over her lips. *Shhhh.*

"What?"

"He's talking again. I have to write it all down." She turned to the mirrors and scratched out another sentence.

"Mom. Mom!"

She snapped around, snarling this time. With her stained black fingers, she reached over and scrawled two words on the glass between them, writing it backwards so there could be no mistaking that it was for him.

SUNDAY RUNDAY

He must have made a face showing his confusion, because she slapped her palms against the glass and wiped away everything but

RUN

"I'm not leaving you!" Sunday remembered the glass break hammer from Honey's glove compartment. He dug it out and whacked the big pane, spiderwebbing the glass.

A great rumbling began and Regina glanced dreamily upward, then leveled her gaze and punched the tip of her finger into the word for emphasis.

"No!" cried Sunday, pushing against the glass with all his strength, only to see the cracks contracting inward. Like it was healing.

Again and again, he struck the glass only to watch its wounds disappear. His mother turned and walked away, ignoring Sunday as he pounded and screamed for her. The floor shook. The lights flickered. If it went dark, his chances of finding his way out would go from slim to impossible. He scrambled along the walls until he found fresh air and went that way. Beyond the walls of the *Un-house*, it sounded like a colossal beast had awakened and was rolling over for a morning stretch.

A voice spoke, full of static and distorted as if through a loudspeaker or bullhorn. Sunday couldn't parse the words. But it was the same voice he'd heard in his vision coming from inside the big top. He pivoted about until he found the direction the voice was loudest, then tried to cut a path through the maze that got him closer to it.

Soon, he was running, ping-ponging along, as the voice became louder and crystalized.

...opening of the Twilight Faire! Come, experience the attractions! Ride the mechanized entertainments! See the Mouse Boy! Try your luck at the Bonebreaker! Fill your belly from one of our many floss wagons, grabs, and poppers! Try our famous waffle-battered hairballs! Shock your tongue on a bone marrow lolly! Caress the skin of the Translucent Woman! Massage the organs of the Diaphanized Man! Run for your lives as you are pursued by our newest acquisition in immersive amusements, the Pork Urchins!

Feeling a wave of even cooler air, Sunday burst from a pair of wooden doors, launching over a set of steps and into the hay-covered ground, knocking his wind out. He rolled over and saw the Faire was in the process of starting up—or more accurately, coming alive. Smoke and exhaust billowed from the huge rides as they began to oscillate and churn.

Come one! Come all! Bring the kids! The family that plays together, stays together! Forever!

Sunday sprinted around the back of the *Un-house* looking for a way to gain access and find his mother. There were more doors, all padlocked. Something rustled underneath the trailer. Sunday leaned into the grass and weeds below, peering into the darkness. A clod of dirt struck him in the face and he reeled backward. Then it was on his chest, blurry through his muddy eyes, some kind of wire-haired animal by the screeching. He seized its neck and tossed it aside, where it quickly regained balance and charged like a feral hog provoked.

Sunday was up and running when the thing latched onto his back. It squealed, scratching and biting. He spun around trying to get a grip on it. From the corner of his eye, he saw others darting between rides and amusements and food carts. They galloped on all fours like their porcine namesakes but giggled like hyenas. He pulled out the Swiss Army Knife and tried to unfold it as another of the little beasts launched from atop the pink asbestos cotton candy stand, knocking him down and sending the knife out of reach. He rolled and recovered, setting off again, now with two of the animals latched to his shoulders and torso by talons and teeth.

Thusly encumbered, he cantered down the midway toward the old latrine. Hulking steel engines chugged to life as he went, sending jagged and rusting fair rides into motion. Desperation kept him from realizing just how hard he was struggling to breathe, and while the jaws of his attackers certainly hurt, the scuba suit was doing an admirable job at keeping them from breaking skin. Didn't apply to his face, though, which was vulnerable to gouging by their little rodent-like hands and ra- zor claws. Sunday skidded to a stop and threw his body down, launching one to the ground. It came at him. He punted it.

His ankle burned as he neared the portable, flesh and muscle cauteriz- ing once more as the parasite went vapor hot. Almost to the outhouse, he was buffeted from the side and fell to the ground. Two more of the hairy bastards latched themselves to his thigh and stomach. A glint of steel and he felt a stab in his ribs. Another in his shoulder. He stood, all furious and bearlike, grabbing at tiny arms and legs and hurling them away like squirrels on a ceiling fan. Sunday slipped, nearly fell into the frontier shitter, and threw the latch just as the varmints launched themselves against the door.

His calf glowed orange, lighting the interior. A glint of steel stuck out from his chest. Half a pair of children's scissors, embedded in his ribs. The other half angled out from his shoulder like a dollar store epaulette. He yanked it free. The toilet hole went ebullient and began to open. The stalk ascended and spread itself wide. Outside, his pursuers whinnied and oinked. They scratched and pounded the door, splitting the wood.

"Fuck it." Sunday said, yanking the second scissor blade from his chest and throwing himself against the membrane.

While his trip through the toilet to the Twilight Faire had been near instantaneous, this was an unguided voyage through some kind of tunnel made of organic tissue. The comparison was obvious, of course. Sunday knew the inside of an asshole when he saw one.

The tunnel began to slope but soon leveled out. Eventually he had to crawl, pulling himself forward like Andy Dufresne of *Shawshank Redemption* fame, only instead of a sewer pipe, he burrowed headlong through actual intestines.

The tunnel rumbled and Sunday found himself propelled ahead as the organ contracted. The next thing he knew, he blasted up and out, hitting the plastic ceiling of a portable and flopping to the floor like a carp off the line.

He righted himself and inspected the tank. A loud sucking noise howled from within. The fleshy pipe disintegrated like an unstable wormhole that dissipates after it forms. Then it was just a tank again.

Sunlight beamed through the vented panels beneath the roof. He turned the latch and pushed on the door, but something held it closed. He bellied into it, cracking it by an inch. Shoving his face to the opening he saw.

"Oh, no." The unit had been wrapped in police tape. *And* he'd lost his tools. Sunday cast about for something else he might use to cut through it. The toilet paper dispenser had a stiff plastic edge. It popped free when he punched it. He stuck it through the crack and pulled down on the tape until it snapped. The door flew open and he rolled out like a buttermilk biscuit.

The portable sat in the rental company's storage yard. Sunday shook his head—damned cops would do anything not to have to store a latrine. Was he still in Mineral Wells? By the look of the unit, it was the very one he'd climbed into over in Palo Pinto County. Where was Honey? How was he going to get home? He'd missed his meeting with Gaynes. Was he now a fugitive? The scuba suit itched like a wool sock full of chiggers, and though his olfactory senses were mostly toast, he was confident in the profundity of his odor.

He tried to organize his mind, figure the next step. But his brain was tossed like the inside of a twister-kissed singlewide. There was his lost mom, a carnival straight out of Hellraiser, the cops, and his pressing need for a bath.

"Oh shit!" he said, digging into the suit's utility pocket. "Shit shit shit!"

He found the baggie with his phone inside, took it out and dialed the one person he knew he could trust with reliable transportation.

Chapter Twelve

Offer of Proof

"Where the hell have you been?" squealed Ms. Poppy. "I've been worried to death."

"Mineral Wells."

"That's it?"

"You drinking?"

"It's seven-thirty a.m."

"That's why I'm asking."

"I'm sober as a judge."

"Alright. Well, Honey's gone. Don't know where she is. Can you come get me?"

"In Mineral Wells?"

"Yeah, I can see Highway one-eighty from here. There's a RV park to the west. I'm in a sanitation lot. I can make it out to the highway."

"On my way."

"Oh. Can you run inside my trailer and grab me a change of clothes and some flippies?"

"Why?"

"Just ... can you, please?"

"Yessir."

Sunday ended the call and marched across the gravel lot where he found a hose inside a cleaning station. The water was colder than icebox booze but getting clean was the more dominant urge than staying warm. He removed his boots and dowsed himself. The stab holes in his ribs and shoulder stung like mesquite thorns, but they should've hurt more than they did. He angled his eye toward the wound in his side and found it was barely there, as if it was healing already. He considered infection but had just been through a tank of biocide and so back burnered the thought. He rinsed the suit too, hating that he'd have to don it again as he couldn't be caught parading out to the highway in the buck.

Groaning, he stretched into the swampy suit and navigated through the lot. The gate was shut so he climbed up the fence. Being a few belt notches out of shape, he lost his grip and fell flat on his back atop a pile of tarps blasting the wind out his lungs. The sky went purple and faded to black, and then it was the mirrored hall, with his mother's story smeared in grease paint. Or maybe he was hallucinating on the brink of passing out.

Catfishing his mouth for breath, he watched as the gate squeaked slowly open until it tapped his foot. He rolled side to side until his diaphragm finally released and gulped the air.

Then there was music and the unmistakable tenor of Tina Turner's voice reassuring someone that they were *simply the best*, and the crunch of tires rolling onto the shoulder. The car idled. The sky flashed to clear blue, and Sunday groaned himself upright.

Ms. Poppy drove a 1994 maroon Pontiac Firebird convertible with a 3.4-liter V6 because she liked to "go fast." Sunday didn't have the heart to tell her that there was a difference between going fast and sounding fast, because the 1994 Firebird was perhaps the greatest living example of a car where noise and speed were inversely related.

"What happened?" she said, laughing as she lowered her horsefly sunglasses. "You remind me of a hitcher I once picked up outside the Monolithic Dome Institute back in the eighties."

Sunday opened the door. "I'm wet."

"Then change." She leaned down for the trunk release. "Got some old towels in back, along with your clothes."

"You're the best, Ms. Poppy."

"You're kinda blue, Sunday. Bleeding too."

"I know," he called over the back window. "Got some puncture wounds, but," he tapped at the one in his shoulder, and almost couldn't find it, "I think they're gonna be okay. Anyway, look, we got a prob—"

"Cops came around asking for you."

Sunday waited for a break in the traffic and quickly peeled away the scuba suit and pulled on a pair of Hawaiian shorts from the 1990s (bad call), a black Motörhead tee (good call), and stepped into a pair of flip flops (fantastic call). Being clean and dry and most importantly alive, he felt a rill of excitement. He'd taken the shitter to hell and found his mother. She wasn't beyond saving. The next time he'd be better prepared and bring them both back.

He came around to the front of the Firebird.

"What'd they say, the cops?"

"They think you ran."

He opened the door and dropped into the seat. "Fuck."

"Why would you run?"

"I didn't run. But they think I did something to my mother. I know where she is. And I think I know where those damned Doucet brats are too. Pretty sure they tried to eat me. *Pork Urchins.*"

Ms. Poppy inspected his face. "Looks like you fought an opossum."

"Something like that. Let's go."

"Where to?"

"Home."

"But the cops."

"I'm not trying to run from the cops. I can show them the truth." He put his foot up on the Firebird's faded red dashboard to display his mangled calf.

Ms. Poppy recoiled. "Oh, hell no. What is that?"

"That's the carnival rabbit I brought home for Mom."

"But—"

"Fuckin' thing was haunted, I swear. I cooked it in the oven and the damned thing crawled up my leg, and now for some reason ... I think it permits me to traverse between realms." He dropped his leg to the floor. "That's where I found Mom."

"In another realm?"

"Hm-mm."

Ms. Poppy dug around in the side pocket of the door, presented a miniature bottle of Fireball, and quickly drank it down. Sunday knew better than to protest, so long as she didn't produce another to chase it. He told her everything as they motored toward Glen Rose, rendering Ms. Poppy speechless for probably the first time in her life.

"And the thing is, I can prove it all to the Donut Shark, Gaynes, when I see him. I can prove that the toilet sitting at my house is a doorway. It took Mom. It probably took those kids."

"So, it isn't all bad."

"Goddamn, Ms. Poppy."

"You said they tried to eat you down there."

Sunday shrugged. Still, they had parents waiting for them here on Earth.

Back in town, Ms. Poppy rolled into a twenty-four-hour clinic. Sunday started to get out of the car but stopped and reached a hand up his shirt to check his wounds. They were healed. He flipped down the visor and considered himself in the makeup mirror. No sign of his quarrel with the urchins whatsoever.

He shrugged. "Let's head home."

A police cruiser was parked in the spot where Sunday usually kept Honey. "Just let me out here," he said, as they pulled in front of his singlewide. Ms. Polly obliged and Sunday got out.

The driver's side door of the cruiser opened and Gaynes unfolded from within like a hermit crab. His gun was drawn but not pointed. He said something into his radio. Sunday put his hands up because that's what you did and hollered, "Unarmed."

"You're wanted. Kidnapping."

"Didn't do it. I can prove it."

"You should have told me that last night when you were only a person of interest. Then you ran. Now you're a suspect. That's how it works."

"Why would I kidnap my own mother?"

"Don't want to guess on it. Could be you're a sicko."

Sunday got a whiff of potent berry smoke and then Ms. Poppy was standing to the right, completing a triangle. "She's down the shitter," she said. "And so are the Doucets. Like a gang of little turds."

"Go back to your trailer Ms. Poppy," said Gaynes without looking at her.

"It's a free country. I'll stand right here. Would serve you to listen some instead of flapping those gums, officer. I told you those kids went down that toilet right behind you. I saw it happen."

That was new to Sunday. It had to be a lie. She was trying to help him.

"I've got your rig over at the impound lot. Got a call that a latrine technician pulled a magic trick up in Mineral Wells. Eyewitnesses. A bunch of carnies—"

"Troupers."

"What?"

"They're called troupers."

"Shut the fuck up. A pack of carnies saw you climb into that unit and when they finally got it open, you were gone. Presto. Sunday fucking Harry Houdini fucking McWhorter."

"You still think I took my mother?"

"I think you're up to something or you wouldn't be performing magic tricks inside them toilets."

"You're not here to arrest me, are you?"

"Why else would I be here?"

"But you believe me?"

"I believe that something isn't adding up and that it's bigger than you, sure." He reached into the cruiser and hung up his radio, then shut the door. "Sixty-two missing persons reports last night. Sixty-two. But that doesn't mean you're not connected to your mother's disappearance."

"Sixty-two!"

"Regionally. That we know of. There's more, no doubt. The strike zone keeps growing. Handful of cases out east past the Pine Curtain. Canton, Longview, and way, way southwest. The work of an organized ring of some kind doing the grabbing. Human trafficking seems the obvious thing."

"Human trafficking for septuagenarians, Gaynes?" exclaimed Sunday. He walked toward his house. Gaynes stiffened. "Let me show you something. Come inside."

His map was still spread across the kitchenette table. Ms. Poppy joined, settling into the door frame like a shift supervisor. Sunday tried to recount everything the museum teen had told him about the County Fair of 1936 and the fiery death of A.V. Cadogan. "He's back and trying to pull as many people into this alternative world as he can."

"And you're saying he's coming in through the port-a-potties?"

"*Portal*-potties. Sorta like *Doctor Who*, except the Tardis is a shitter."

"Tardis?"

"Goddamn, Gaynes, like a time machine."

The cop stared blankly then shook his head. "You say you can prove it? Prove it."

Sunday grabbed his last geotag from the table. "Come on." He led them outside to the portable and handed his phone to Gaynes. "See the dot? That's this tag right here." The deputy nodded. Sunday opened the door to the unit and tossed the tag into the tank.

"It's just sitting there."

"Yeah," said Sunday, crossing his arms. "That's what it does."

Gaynes marched toward the latrine.

"Eh, eh, I wouldn't do that. There's a chance we've already summoned it and you get yourself snatched. Maybe just let me do it." Sunday gestured to the now burning hot relic wound up his calf.

"Heck is that?" said the cop.

Sunday tapped the phone. "Just watch the screen."

Gaynes nodded.

Sunday walked slowly toward the unit and stopped at the door. Gaynes called from behind. "Nothing yet."

"How about now?" Sunday stepped into the portable.

All color leached from the cop's face.

"What?"

"It moved. Damned thing moved."

Sunday hopped out and faced the deputy. "And where did it go? Wait. Let me guess. Dublin."

"Dublin."

Chapter Thirteen

Fireball in the Kitchenette

"Well," said Gaynes, shifting his hips.

"Well?" said Sunday.

"I mean, it's all very interesting. Even if you're right, I don't think this particular phenomenon falls under my jurisdiction. Federal Bureau, possibly."

"The hell it doesn't. My mother's gone. And I located your missing teen with no face. He's down there running the *Skinner*."

"He's alive?"

Sunday's mind flashed to Roy all cut to shit and the funnel-cake girl with no guts. "Yep."

"You keep saying 'down there'," said the deputy.

"Feels like some kind of hell is all."

"Hmm. Not sure if the police powers extend to parallel dimensions."

Sunday glared. "They seem to extend everywhere else."

Gaynes allowed the insult to pass as it was mostly true. "Well, this is all a little ... overwhelming to be honest. Some eighty people reported missing across twentyish counties and showing no signs of slowing down."

"My source in Dublin said Cadogan vowed to bring his Faire back to life one day. Looked to me like he'd collected nearly enough people to run the show. Now he needs to fill it with customers."

"Then what?"

Sunday shrugged.

"Why does this Dublin teen of yours know so much?" said Gaynes.

Ms. Poppy billowed smoke. "She works in a museum all about Dublin."

"Are all the missing persons coming from county fairs?" asked Sunday.

"Yeah, and the like. Traveling carnivals, pumpkin patches, hayrides, haunted houses. The panoply of autumn's various celebrations."

"So, get them shut down. That's the only way to starve Cadogan out. Can't take people that aren't there."

"The State of Texas has a great many powers at its disposal, but shutting down seasonal entertainments from Alpine to Marshall is a tall order."

"That's rich," said Ms. Poppy, sending up a column of smoke like Old Faithful.

"What's that supposed to mean?" said Gaynes, his belly rolling like a beachball under his shirt.

"Y'all banned books state-wide. Y'all banned abortions state-wide." She scoffed. "Ban the tilt-a-whirl, coward."

"Hey, now. That wasn't me."

"Oh, yeah?" she blew a plume right at him. "Who'd you vote for?"

"Guys!" said Sunday.

"I don't have the pull to get every damned carnival and pumpkin patch in the state shut down, especially on the basis of your working theory."

"It's the truth."

"I believe *something*," said Gaynes. "And I don't really know what. But only after seeing it with my own eyes. The kidnappings are gaining steam in the news cycle. It's undeniable that something is up."

"The news won't stop people from going," said Sunday.

Gaynes nodded somberly. "I hear that. Nobody thinks it'll be them until it is." He gazed at the portable and tapped Sunday's phone on the side. "Could we maybe send something down there through the portal? A bomb?"

"What are you saying right now?"

"He doesn't have a bomb," said Ms. Poppy, as if there were a scenario where he might.

"I obviously know the way in and the way out. Maybe I go back and try to find Cadogan."

"You're still a suspect."

"Okay fine. That doesn't mean you have to arrest me."

"Oh, I have to arrest you."

"Why?"

Gaynes slapped his hands on his hips. "I wanted to talk to you. You fled!"

"I came back."

"Come on. You can ride in front. I won't cuff you." He pivoted to Ms. Poppy. "If you want to be his friend, follow me to the station and help him post bail." He looked at his watch. "The judge is usually a little tipsy by the afternoon arraignments. I'll tell him you're not a flight risk. Get lucky, you'll be out on your own recognizance by this evening."

"Can't you tell them what you saw?" Sunday demanded, gesturing at the evidence portable as if it was the Colossus of Rhodes. "What I just showed you?"

"I've found," said Gaynes, snorting and then gathering his thoughts, "that to report extranormal encounters as a basis for the commission of State felonies is to place one's standing within the department, and indeed the very welfare of one's pension, into substantial jeopardy. You'll forgive me if there's no checkbox on our forms for the ghost of a dust bowl era carnival baron returning from the dead to resurrect his traveling show."

Gaynes took Sunday through booking at the Somervell County Jail. To his surprise, the danged Donut Shark did him a favor, charging him only with obstructing an official investigation rather than the full kidnapping rap, and Ms. Poppy was able to keep her engine running while he was processed through. But it was clear the clock was ticking. Gaynes wished him luck but said that if he didn't return by his arraignment in three days with either his mother or something more than ghost stories and geotags, then he'd be booked for kidnapping complete with all the fixings.

Back home, Sunday sat across from Ms. Poppy in the kitchenette like he and his mother had done so many times before. He absently twiddled one of her scrunchies between his fingers. He felt numb. Helpless.

Pushing the scrunchie to his nose, he smelled her. She could have been right there with them.

Poppy poured them each a dose of Fireball.

"Drink."

He obeyed, stifling a cough as the devil's syrup stripped his throat.

"You're a great son. Your mom knows that. Any mother would be blessed to have you."

Sunday nodded. "Yeah well—"

"Stop that. You're not perfect. No one is. But you love her unequivocally."

He spun the glass between his fingers. "Mind if I ask you a personal question?"

"There comes a time in your life when you start hoping people will ask you things just to give you the chance to talk. What is it?"

"You have kids, huh?"

"Hmm-mm."

"What do they—where are they at?"

"Oh, that's a tale, isn't it?" She gave herself another pour as if it were fuel to get her through it. "All I'll say is, *I tried*. I did what I thought was right at every turn. You don't know what's right and then all of a sudden, you're a mother. There's no guidebook, no manual for every situation. But my mistakes took their toll, I suppose. One here, one there. They added up. I've always had my demons. I vowed I wouldn't repeat the mistakes of my parents and for the most part, I didn't. But there was enough of them in me, and a bit of that must've seeped through during my weaker moments. People get stubborn, prideful, stop talking to each other. Say things that there's no coming back from. We were all guilty of that. And then, there's the silence. It gets longer and deeper. A big gorge that's impossible to cross."

"You can't have a conversation?"

"Now there's something I've thought about every day for years. No lie. And you know what I've had to admit to myself?"

Sunday shook his head.

Ms. Poppy's eyes gleamed like the wet in her glass. "I realized that I don't like who they became, and that it's truly my fault. I'm to blame for it and I can't undo it." She rubbed her eyes. "They were perfect little babies and if I had made better choices, they would have been better people and I'd ..."

Love them. Sunday knew what she'd stopped herself from saying. "It's okay, Ms. Poppy. It's amazing any of us get along with anyone else, even family. You tried your best."

"I said I tried, that's all. I know there were times I didn't try my best because I was selfish or distracted or whatever. Inattentive. I hope they can forget me, to be honest. I hope they've found people in their lives that can help them be the better people that I wasn't able to make them." She finished the Fireball and spun the cap onto the bottle with an expert flourish.

"You can't blame yourself for everything. There's not always a reason. Sometimes folks just don't work out."

"Yeah. Maybe. Hey, when was the last time you slept?"

Sleep didn't feel like it was part of Sunday's life anymore. He shook his head.

"Come on," she said, going to the door to his room. "If you've got the strength to manage, get in there and lay down. You'll be no good to anyone if you're a zombie. We'll figure this out together once you're rested."

Sunday didn't argue. He shuffled in and angled over the foot of his bed, falling face first into the sheets the surface of a pond.

Chapter Fourteen

Do You Want Me to Rot?

His dreams were a swirling mess of scenes from the real world and the Twilight Faire. He dreamt of a midway expanding like the road into an ancient city. Alexandria or Babylon. He dreamt in vivid detail of awful new attractions. The *Human Skeleton*, the *Camel Girl*, the *Enervator Elevator / Old-Timey Nerve Lifter*, *The Masochist*. He dreamt that the big top was burrowing up from the ground in both places, binding Cadogan's shadow realm to that of the living, then slowly becoming stronger until it was real again, and powerful, unstoppable. A Forever Faire of pain and agony and custom-tailored horrors. Revenge. On everyone.

He dreamt the sensation of water droplets on his toes. A repetitive *pat, pat, pat*, upon his thin bedsheet, each one soaking through to his skin. He rolled over, shifting, now slightly awake and thinking only how real the wetness felt before drifting off again. His eyes cracked and his mom was there.

"Sunday?"

He shot up, pushing back and slamming his headboard against the wall.

"I'm sorry," she said from the foot of the bed. "I couldn't think of a way to wake you that wouldn't frighten."

She wore her regular nightgown and for a moment Sunday thought it had all been a nightmare. But her hair hung long and heavy, sopping. Another drip glinted in the moonlight as it found his covers. He reached for the light.

"No, please, my eyes aren't used to all that."

Sunday pressed his vision into the shadows made by her hair. He could see the orange paint of her face even in the wan light.

"How did you get out?"

"I was never a captive. I was a guest. I am a guest. I was shown."

"You can't go back."

"Sundaaaaaay," she pouted. "Don't say that. I didn't come back here to escape. I came back for you. I've made it so we can be there together."

"What are you talking about?"

She smiled, her highlighter yellow teeth glowing in the dark. "I have my mind back again. You saw it in the *Un-house*, my whole life written out. The Faire is such a charmed and magical place. But to keep what was lost, I have to stay there on the grounds. Anywhere else and it all just unravels for me."

"The *place* is some type of hell."

"Hell is knowing you're losing your mind and watching it go. I hope you never learn that."

"I know enough of hell watching you suffer."

"My sunny child," she said, reaching for one of his feet, which he jerked away. "I don't suffer anymore." The yellow smile disappeared, and her mouth turned down. "I can't stay here. I can feel the fabric of who I am loosening. That terrible disease took more than my mind. It's taken you away from me. You read the mirrors. You saw what I'd kept from you all those years. The truth about your father and my family. What I went through to hold onto you, to protect you. I want to be with my son, but here I won't know you. I will forget you entirely. I will forget myself. And soon, it will all come apart." She crawled up from the foot of the bed, her wet hair leaving tracks in the sheets as she came face to face with him. "Come with your mother. Be with me, my darling child, my sunny day, my everything."

Sunday slipped out from beneath her and off the bed. "No. You don't even know what that place really is. It's not good. Is it even on this planet?"

"It's in Dublin," she said, sitting on the bed.

"It's not in the Dublin that's there right now. I was in Dublin two days ago."

She leaned back on her knees. "Oh Sunday, Sunny-Deeeee. It will be in Dublin and in Glen Rose and Dallas and New York and Shanghai! The Twilight Faire will be all there is!"

"When?"

She stood on the bed and did a jig, flouncing her gown as if it were royal finery. "I'm just so happy! Look at me! When was the last time you saw me like this? Doo-dee-doo."

Tears streamed down Sunday's face. He shook his head. She kept at it, bouncing side to side, her crooked yellow grin of candy corn teeth growing wider with each step.

"Oopsie," she said, ceasing her dance and looking down at the bed to a gathering puddle of urine. Her face pinched to anger. "See? I've had an accident. I can't do it. I can't stay!" She pounced to the floor like a cat stalking a cockroach.

"I love you, but you can't go back. I can't let you go back." He navigated himself toward the door and shut it.

Her face was that of a child's, confused and fearful, her voice full of hurt. "What are you doing?"

"You're going to stay here with me. I'll take care of you. I'll bring in professionals."

"PROFESSIONALS!" Her shining teeth became momentarily sharp, as if they'd been filed. "I'm not going to be stuffed in a cabinet at Bluebonnet Springs Nursing Home! I won't stay and rot in this place. Even if you won't come with me."

He put his hands out, trying to calm her. "Now, let's talk about it."

"Do you want me to rot?" Her face grew pallid, and sores opened in her cheeks, leaking black blood and white-yellow puss. Her lips peeled by layers and sloughed away, leaving the long-enameled, yellow grin. She opened her mouth wide, wide enough to fall into, then began to whine.

"Mom?"

Her eyes pushed from their sockets and bloomed like onions on the flame. The whine amplified into an ear-splitting howl. A harpy's shriek. Sunday covered his ears and braced as the walls of his home vibrated. She stopped screaming, letting the sound die in her throat like a storm siren winding down, shut her mouth, and but for the yellow teeth and orange paint, returned to her normal self. She gracefully swept her hair behind her ears. "I would never make you do something you didn't want to do."

Sunday saw that vision of her again, standing on the ceiling of the mirrored corridor. His fingertips shook. Fear. But not fear in the way of being scared for life and limb. Fear of reality, of what was happening to his mother—of where she'd been and where she wanted to go. Fear of what would happen if he let her. Of what would happen if he didn't. She'd told him what she wanted and seemed—strangely—in her right mind. How could he not respect that? Except that respecting it meant allowing her to return to a sadist's fever dream. Autonomy needed limits. Wasn't walking into hell one of them?

He shook his head. "No. I'll take another job. I'll pay for the best care. Maybe they'll find a cure—"

She shoved her thumb into his mouth, hooking it against his palate. "When you were a baby, you loved this. Do you love it now, Sunday?"

He groaned and flailed, trying to escape, but she had him trapped in the corner of the room. She was strong. He couldn't budge.

"You don't love it now, though, I can tell." She yanked the finger from his mouth. "Sit. SIT!"

He slumped down the wall.

"I will be waiting for you. But I can't let you stop me." She squatted in front of him and a stream of urine pattered the tile as she began to sing. The puddle expanded, touching his toes as she reached the chorus. The song was only distantly familiar, but he remembered it.

> *Sleep, baby, sleep*
> *Your father tends the sheep*
> *Your mother shakes the dream-*
> *land tree*
> *And from it fall sweet dreams for*
> *thee*
> *Sleep, baby, sleep*
> *Sleep, baby, sleep.*

And he did.

The DFW Morning Telegram.com

Human Trafficking Ring Claims Hundreds Across Central Texas and Surrounds

Gretel Van Haemer—Regional Staff Reporter

Recent kidnappings have brought a new breed of fear to Spooky Season. With Halloween still three weeks away, police and sheriff's departments around the state are working non-stop to get a handle on who is behind the abductions and how those responsible have been able to do it without leaving a trace.

With over forty counties affected and almost three hundred reported missing, Governor Gary Abner held a press conference to declare a state of emergency. "These kidnappings seem to center around community fairs, carnivals, and the like. Most victims reported leaving to visit the temporary toilet facilities and never returned. People need to steer clear and stay home. Do not treat this like a game or you might end up in a shipping container or a radical leftist's sex dungeon."

Pressed for details on these claims, Gov. Abner stated that he was just speaking from "common gut-sense" but offered no further information.

The DFW Morning Telegram.com will continue to update the story as it develops.

Chapter Fifteen

Kin

A beam of midmorning sun blazed Sunday's eyelid, snapping him up from where he'd crumpled during the night. A strike of pain flashed down his neck as his head had been wedged sideways into the corner of the room.

He patted down his sheets, hoping to prove it was all a dream, but his fingers settled upon the wet spot in the center of the mattress. He ricocheted through the kitchenette and out the front door, calling for his mother. Rounding the corner of his home, he tripped over Ms. Poppy's Rascal, which lay on its side and thumped onto the ground in front of the portable. The butt of a strawberry-scented cigar sat in a patch of blackened grass.

He called out. "Ms. Poppy?" Even as he stormed into her home, he knew. And for the first time in the whole damned situation, he felt a real sense of focused anger. Maybe his mother had sought to provide him with stronger motivation to follow her back into the Faire. She'd been wrong to do it. Involving Ms. Poppy was unforgivable. She didn't deserve what awaited her in that place.

Outside, Sunday prepared to summon the ghoulish toilet thing that would pull him below. The haunted rabbit eel was already warming up on his leg, but he stopped shy. He'd be flying blind. He'd barely gotten out alive on his first trip and he hardly knew how the place worked, where Ms. Poppy would be, or how to deal with Cadogan. He needed to be smart. There was no guarantee he could get everyone back home safe.

Inside Ms. Poppy's trailer, he located the keys to her Firebird. Then he launched down the highway louder than he was fast.

The sky over Dublin was as purple as a bruise. Sunday had to turn on the Firebird's lights even though it was barely noon. He slowed as he made his way through town. People moseyed about as if it was a normal day, many with their sunglasses on. But his calf burned like the whole town was infected by Cadogan's spell.

The Firebird's brakes squealed the car to a stop outside the Dublin Historical Showroom and Guided Audio Tour. Sunday ran inside. "Gabriela? Gabby?"

A curtain in the back swooped open and Gabby appeared in a jean jacket with black skirt over black stockings and colossal blue glitter Doc Martens. "Hey there! What's up? Lose your squashed penny?"

"No, I—" he hesitated, then pulled the penny up from his big chest pocket where she'd once put it.

"Ha, cool."

Sunday gestured to her outfit. "You going somewhere?"

"Oh, yeah. I'm off today."

"Oh, um."

"*Was* off today. Dad had to go to Lampasas for a llama."

"Y'all raise llamas?"

"*He* raises llamas." She leaned against the doorframe.

"You look like you're dressed up for something."

"Oh, do I?"

"Sorry, don't want to pry." He had a feeling.

"Me and some friends are going to Stephenville."

"Why you going to Stephenville?"

"The fair."

"You serious? Haven't you heard about the kidnappings?

She raised her eyebrows. "Yeah. It makes it more exciting. They're not gonna snatch us out of a crowd."

"They ain't pulling people from crowds," he said. "Look, I'm a latrine technician. Last week"—*was it only last week?*—"I was doing maintenance on the portables up in Glen Rose—"

"Portapotties?"

"I prefer 'latrine' or 'port-o-let,' but yes. Anyhow, I found the face of a missing teen named Roy West Carpenter in the waste tank. I found the rest of him yesterday."

"Where?"

"In Cadogan's Twilight Faire. Roy was running *The Skinner*."

Gabby's facial expression didn't change. Had she not heard him or blocked him out?

"Hello?"

Gabby's gaze dropped to the floor, and she ran her hair behind her ear. "So, he kept his promise."

"Yes. Yes! Exactly. Wait," said Sunday, hooking a thumb into the strap of his coveralls. "Wait. Are you messing with me?"

"No," said Gabby, spinning away. "Come with me."

He followed her through the maroon curtain to the back room. Similar to the front room, there were glass display cases with artifacts and photos. She led him through a maze of old banker's boxes overflowing with papers. "What's all this?"

Gabby flipped a switch on the wood paneled wall, which lit the display cases from the inside. "Apocrypha."

"I don't ... what do you mean?"

"How long have you lived in Glen Rose?"

"Eighth grade."

"So, you know these small towns. People talk. Everybody knows everybody else's business. And the worst part is, they feel like it's their right to know. They feel entitled. And if you slip, if you're different, you do something that doesn't fit their preferred image of the place, their narrative, you're done."

Sunday shrugged. "Well, yeah."

Gabby moved down the display, folded over some dusty blankets on the top. "My point is, there's more to the Twilight Faire than what's out in the main room. The stuff that would really embarrass Dublin is in here. The truth. All the crap that would have us run out of town if we displayed it."

"Cadogan was the boss of a traveling carnival. How could Dublin be judged for what he did or what happened at the Faire?"

Gabby smiled. It seemed sad. "After all that happened, the massacre, to know that Cadogan's family never left town. It would be too much."

"Hold on. I'm confused. Are you saying—"

"Here." She led Sunday to a section of the case stacked with photographs. There was Cadogan, seated tall in a chair with his wife and a trio of children standing behind. Two girls and a boy, all under ten.

Sunday tapped the glass and looked from the picture to Gabby, who hadn't let her gaze leave his face. "What are you trying to tell me?"

"Well, that one, the younger girl on the right? Her name was Edna Elaine Cadogan and she had a little boy and then he had a little boy—my father. Which means—"

"You're a Cadogan."

"Well, Elaine married, so I'm a Fuentes. But yeah, A.V. Cadogan is my great-great-grandfather."

"And no one in Dublin knows this?"

"Some do, probably. The olds with barns full of tractors and lawn jockeys. Everyone is just waiting for the history to die out. Most of all, *us*."

"Why didn't your family just leave?"

Gabby turned and leaned back on the case, stared at the curtained door and sighed.

Sunday guessed. "Because you can't?"

"Mm-hm, that's right."

"How? How can he keep you here?"

"His curse. He's got us on an invisible chain or rope."

"I saw something like that when I was down there. The troupers can venture only so far from their spots. He did that to his own family? How far does it extend? How far can you get from Dublin before you're tugged back?" But then he knew. "Lampasas."

Gabby nodded.

"Your whole family? Ever since the uprising?"

"Mm-hm."

"Goddamn."

"How is he coming through?"

"Well, like I said, he's using portables. Mobile latrines."

"Fitting."

"That's why no one has found the kidnapping ring. There isn't one. He's taking people right out of the toilet. My mother's down there, and so is ..." *what was Ms. Poppy to him, really?* "... my other mother."

"Oh no."

"Well, I'm going back. I thought to come down here and talk to you before I flushed myself half-cocked. But I don't have much time. Mom is, well, I'm losing her. She has dementia. There's something about the Faire that lets her have her memories back. She wants to stay. She says the Faire will be everywhere soon. I think it's true. The sky—"

"—you brought up the sky last time. What about the dang sky?"

Sunday rushed out onto the street and pointed. "You don't see that it's entirely dark out here?"

Gabby squinted. "No. It's like lunchtime."

"Yeah, lunchtime at night. It's my parasite I bet."

"Your what?"

Sunday lifted the leg of his coveralls.

Gabby recoiled. "What is that?"

"That is the cremated remnant of a big old stuffed rabbit I found leaning against the portable through which Roy Carpenter and his lady friend were sucked. It was *his* face that came off. Not sure about the friend but the rabbit was possessed. I lit it on fire and the rest is history."

"Your leg doesn't look so good."

Sunday didn't care to linger on the amalgam of his flesh and the bedeviled remains, but on Gabby's comment he unfortunately did. The blackened serpent had tightened its coil, trenching deeper into the muscle of his calf. The margins were swollen hot with infection and oozing profusely. He dropped the pant leg.

"Have you tried getting it off?"

"It ain't coming off. And for now, I need it. It's sort of my ticket in and out of the Faire. And I think it lets me see all that." He washed his hand across the sky. "When I traveled there, it was here, in Dublin. In the city park. It feels like it's trying to push through."

"That's what Cadogan promised when they burned him. A return of the Twilight Faire."

"I need to know how to fight him."

"Your plan is to fight him?"

"Probably not as fast as I used to be, but I'm good in a scrap. Plus, Ms. Poppy's got a pistol in her glove compartment."

"Who?"

"The other mom."

Gabby headed through the curtain into the showroom. "I don't think a gun is gonna do much for you in there."

Sunday followed. "Well, okay. That's why I'm here. I need to figure out the angle in case there's a confrontation as I'm trying to get my moms out."

Gabby stopped beside a stack of boxes. "I have an idea."

Chapter Sixteen

Just Like Big Tex

G abby unstacked the boxes until she created a bare spot on the old hardwoods and the clear outline of a door.

"We have a few of his things," said Gabby, lifting the hatch with a creak.

"Do what?"

"Obviously he didn't live at the Faire with the troupers. He always took lodgings in whatever town the Faire had come to. As a result, none of his stuff was lost to the fire, just time." Gabby exposed the top of a flat trunk covered in buckles and metal fittings. "Help me up with it, eh?"

"Feels sorta like we're messing with the Ark of the Covenant. Doesn't it?"

"The what?"

"Come on. *Indiana Jones*?"

"Ah, of course. A movie from like twenty years before I was born. I've been through this thing a million times," laughed Gabby. "It's not cursed. Far as I know."

Sunday knelt and helped her heave the trunk onto the floor. "What's in here?"

Gabby popped the latches. "Mainly stuff his wife kept. Beryl Louise. I get the feeling they bounced around the county trying to escape the wrath of the population after everything went down. She or one of my great-grandparents eventually circled back to Dublin. Maybe it was the most familiar. Or maybe he drew them in. I don't know. Anyway, there's some old show bills in here, ledgers. A few clothes. Knick-knacks."

She opened it and Sunday nearly gagged. "Smells like shit!"

Gabby waved her hand before her face. "It goes away."

The air took on a purple tinge. "I think you're wrong about it not being cursed, kid."

Gabby shrugged. "I'm trapped in central Texas. I probably wouldn't notice."

Her fingers seized upon something folded into a bolt of exquisitely embroidered velvet and unwrapped it. A book, bound in leather, a clear one-off type of situation with a buckle and a lock.

"Necronomicon," said Sunday.

"No. This isn't *Army of Darkness* ... and you aren't Bruce Campbell. Did you see any movies that came out after the 1980s?"

"*Army* was 1992."

"Okay, boomer."

"I'm Gen-X."

She rolled her eyes. "Anyway. This is Cadogan's journal. It's full of all kinds of crazy shit, but mostly it contains his plans for the next evolution of the Twilight Faire. The one he never got to see come to fruition." She flipped through the pages, searching for an entry. "You said one of the missing persons was operating a ride."

"Yeah."

She opened the book and spun it around so he could see. Sunday about fell over. There was a pen and ink drawing, almost like a blueprint, of the ride he'd seen the teen Roy West Carpenter emerge from. "*Skinner*" was written in blood above the drawing. All of it was written in blood.

"That's exactly what I saw ... I ..."

"Yeah, that's how I knew you weren't dicking around with me. You were really there. Not in the old Twilight Faire. The new." She flipped the pages with more sketches of rides, attractions, games of chance, refreshments, all annotated like building plans. Sunday gasped a little when he saw the *Perpetual Wheel*, *Doom Bingo*, the *Human Fly*, the *Gut Scrambler*—

"Stop," said Sunday.

"What is it?"

"The *Un-house* is where he's got my mom."

"You saw her inside?"

He nodded.

"I'm sorry, man. I'm really sorry."

"It's a giant torture fest. He couldn't have actually built any of this in the real world, so what was he doing? Fantasizing? Sick fuck."

Gabby nodded and closed the book, setting it aside. She dug back into the trunk. Out came a long ringmaster's coat, scarves in many colors, and goggles. Lots of goggles. They were heavy, with side-shields and inky black lenses.

"Was he a welder?" asked Sunday.

"Elaborate sunglasses, more like. You saw the picture in the display out front. Not a fan of sunlight." She had a molded leather pouch in her hands. "Huh." She held it to her ear, then opened the clasp. Out slid a tiny gold pocket watch. It was ticking.

"Okay, well that's new," she said.

"Did you wind it up?"

"I haven't dug around in this thing for years, so no."

"What time does it say?"

She opened the shell. "Uh, four thirty."

"A.m. or p.m.?"

"It's an antique pocket watch, it doesn't specify."

"Right. Seven and a half hours to midnight, or noon, whichever."

Gabby frowned. "It's running backward."

"Backward? Toward what? It's a countdown, isn't it?"

"Not everything is an eighties movie."

"Lookit, that watch is running by itself and going backward. I don't care what era of movies it is. That's a countdown. And my moms are still trapped. You said you had an idea. What?"

"Yeahhhhhh, so." She closed the trunk and threw the latches. "The idea is: I'm coming with you."

"Ahhh—no."

Gabby shot upright. "Ahhh, *yes*. My family has been trapped here like prisoners for almost a hundred years."

"I am not taking responsibility for any more teens in the netherworld. Maybe if your dad was here, he could go."

"First of all, I'm twenty-one. Secondly, I don't need *the patriarchy* to be responsible for me. Third, he and I don't exactly see eye to eye on things. I know more about Cadogan than you or my dad. He pretends the curse isn't real. He doesn't study this shit like I have. He raises llamas."

"Right."

"So let's be clear: inside the Twilight Faire, I'm the adult. *You're* the teen."

Sunday didn't have a whole lot to say to that.

"When do we leave? Like you said, clock's tickin'."

"Soon as possible," he answered, still processing being saddled with a partner. "You might want to change into something more … um," he cleared his throat. "The ingress and egress to the Faire is very sewage-forward."

"Where's the entrance?"

"Now, hold on a second. Before I—ur, we—go back inside, I need to know this guy. What makes Cadogan tic? Strengths, weaknesses. How do we defeat him?"

"He didn't put that in his diary." She held up a finger. "*But.* I've read all his stuff front to back. I know a few things. It's well documented that when he ran the Twilight Faire during his life, he could always be found near *The Ape of Sky*, so we need to find that—"

"The Ape of What?"

"It was a riff on King Kong, which had come out just three years earlier. Cadogan was all about one-upmanship. Except instead of coming from an island, *The Ape of Sky* came from another planet. A giant alien monkey thing. Cadogan claimed it was real, of course, the victim of a spaceship crash, and charged extra to allow folks behind the curtain to see it." She reached through the back of a display case and pulled out a photograph.

"Oh, hell that's terrifying!" Sunday hadn't expected the scale or detail that Cadogan had executed. And it wasn't the gorilla he'd envisioned either, more akin to one of those lanky, long-limbed primates. A gibbon or the like. A macaque maybe. There was an uncanny quality to it. A lengthening of the skull, the exaggerated hunch of its crenellated spine, the angle of head on neck, and length of claws on fingers that made it familiar but undoubtedly not of Earth. It was better than forty feet tall and poised atop a plinth on back feet and front knuckles, ready to pounce.

"How did they transport that thing?"

"Railcar."

"Was it just a statue? What'd it do?"

"Sort of like Big Tex at the State Fair. Stationary but with some animatronics."

"Did the Ape of Sky burn down like Big Tex?"

"When the Troupers put the place to the torch, it did. All that remained was the steel skeleton."

"Just like Big Tex. Okay, well I didn't see an Ape from Venus or any other planet when I was in the shit. What else do you know?"

"His diaries read like a manifesto. Most of it is garbage. If I think of something relevant, you'll be the first one to know."

Sunday turned to leave.

"Hey, where are you going?"

"Thanks for the stroll through history, kid, but I can't let you come with me. You have a life here. I'm sorry about your being leashed to the place, but I just can't stomach being responsible for someone else. I already lost two people."

"You have to take me or you won't beat him."

"I'll risk it."

"You hear me? *You* can't hurt him. Only I can."

"Why's that?"

"You don't know much about blood curses, do you? I'm blood. You're not. I have to do it."

"That's convenient."

"It's true. Sorry."

Sunday scratched his cheeks. People were always surprising him with little pockets of knowledge held in secret. His mother had a wide-ranging insight of the local flora. Ms. Poppy was the unofficial electrician for Live Oaks Enclave. He knew everything there was to know about the early metal scene and its various figureheads, such as Lemmy Kilmister. Why couldn't any of that knowledge be of practical use? Maybe he should have spent more time listening to black metal to cultivate an aptitude for witchcraft. "Explain. Quick."

"It's sort of sorcery 101. But also, he's detailed it in his journals. Cadogan had to break a curse once himself, a 'binding charm' like the one he put on my family. It's how he got out of his native country, Ireland. He tried throwing bodies at the problem before he figured out he had to break it himself. That's what his journals say, anyway."

Sunday knew nothing of spells or charms and had no way to counter what she was saying. If she was right, then he had to let her go with. "You're not bullshitting?"

Gabby picked up a black leather backpack from behind the counter. "We should get snacks."

"They got funnel cake down there, but you wouldn't want to eat it."

Chapter Seventeen

Mirage

G abby just about fell over when they stepped outside. "Whoa, what the hell?"

"Ah, you can see it, now?"

She cranked her neck to the sky. "How could I not?"

Sunday gestured to the pocket watch on Gabby's belt. "That thing is haunted. You weren't wearing it before and now you are and you can see. It's like my thing." He patted his pant leg. "Here, hand me the watch."

Gabby drew it from the pouch and dropped it into his hand, then immediately shielded her eyes.

"Yep," said Sunday, returning the timepiece. "And now?"

"Like midnight. Only purplish." She stared at the sky. "No stars."

They went around the corner to the Allsup's gas station. Sunday's stomach burbled loud enough for Gabby to hear, though she didn't take any visible notice. The station's burritos were legendary but came with a natural consequence he didn't want to have to navigate while inside the dark carnival. He opted for a corndog that tasted like it'd been turning in the warmer since antebellum. A pink plank of Laffy Taffy drooped from between Gabby's teeth as she loaded two entire boxes of it into her backpack.

On the way to the car, Sunday patted at the pockets on his coveralls for the various knives he'd hooked inside. He didn't want to stab a kid, but he felt justified that whatever the Doucet spawn had become inside Cadogan's world were fair game. He selected one, a little pigsticker he'd bought from a gas station in Ozona and offered it to Gabby. She accepted the knife with a grunt as if she'd expected to be provisioned. "This the biggest you got?"

Sunday led the way to the Firebird and got in. Gabby stopped before opening the door. "Getting in a stranger's car and I don't even know where I'm going."

"Dublin City Park. Get in."

She did, setting the pack in her lap.

"Seatbelt."

"It's only like a mile."

He waited.

Gabby rolled her eyes and buckled up. Sunday started the engine and hit the lights, then pulled onto the road.

"So, we're the only ones driving at night," said Gabby as cars passed them going the other way, lights off.

"The way I see it, you and me are a little bit in both worlds right now. Betwixt and between. Me with my parasite and you with your watch. Tokens that let us walk either side of the line."

"Is it like this everywhere?"

"No. Last time I was here though, the sky wasn't so dark. And the perimeter of this purple area didn't reach much beyond your showroom.

Now the whole city is full covered by it as you can see." They rode along until Sunday slowed and made his turn at the metal chicken.

A glow appeared on the horizon like the kind made by a city you drive into at night.

"What's that?"

"That'll be the Faire, I guess."

Uncanny lights and shapes came into view as they approached. Sunday let up on the brakes and the Firebird rolled to a stop. "Well, that's, uh ... hey, can you see that?"

Gabby nodded.

The dead grass field of Dublin City Park was a carnival of phantoms. Ethereal tents, attractions, and rides twinkled in a slow-moving dreamscape. There were no people that Sunday could register, but then again maybe they were all tucked away in their machines waiting for the crowds. Or perhaps they couldn't be seen from this side of the veil. The abandoned portable sat at the distant end of the field, seeming to sit squarely in both worlds. It was still on its side from when Sunday barreled into it.

Gabby shifted in the passenger seat. She set the timepiece on the dash and immediately covered her eyes. "It's all gone now. Just same old Dublin in the daytime. Ugh." She retrieved the watch and sighed.

They parked beneath the patch of trees.

"So, do we just walk out there? How do we get in?"

Sunday pushed open the convertible's door and levered himself out. Leaning across the top of the windshield, he pointed to the distant portable. "You see that crapper downrange?"

"Yeah."

"Well."

"Oh, wow. You were serious about the port-a-potty situation."

"Hmm."

They walked through the trees to the edge of the field to the ghostly, glowing main entrance of the Twilight Faire. Together, they reached for the iron of the elaborate front gate, but their fingers met no resistance. Gabby checked her hand. "I guess I was expecting ectoplasm or something."

"Wait."

They entered onto the midway. It was a strange sensation to feel the crunch of grass below their boots while the ground of the Faire appeared to be mostly dirt and mud. Once inside, the rides seemed to be operating even though any riders were invisible. And it was quiet. Unsettling. Like being spawned inside a reel of a silent movie.

The Faire had expanded. New tents had risen, surrounded by food stands and grisly rides and attractions that weren't there during Sunday's previous visit. Gabby's pace slowed as they passed the *Palace of Organs*, a floss wagon specializing in "pickled guts with crème fraiche," and the *Hang-go-Round*. The ride's center hub turned, twirling a dozen, noose-laden ropes. They were taut, as if swinging invisible passengers by the neck.

"Sunday, are there ... people *in* those?"

He grunted and walked on, double-time. "Lot's more people missing since I was here last."

Gabby sprinted to catch up. "Are they being killed?"

"Last time it just seemed like torture. One of the teens told me she couldn't die. But I don't know. You don't have to come."

"I'm the only one—"

Sunday spun around. "I heard you! I don't really give a shit about Cadogan and blood curses! I'm doing this to bring back my mother and Ms. Poppy. You can stay and fight him for all I care." He stomped ahead.

They passed through the bones of the Twilight Faire's macabre spine until they reached the yellow portable. Sunday pushed it upright. Up close, the planks of the old, wooden mobile latrine were superimposed like a slideshow projection. Touching the door it felt like every other molded plastic door he'd ever handled. It was the same inside, a mix of old and new, not entirely either.

Sunday's parasite burned. He held the door open and ushered Gabriela inside.

"What's gonna happen? Will it hurt? Is it scary?"

"Yep."

Accepting this without further complaint, she stepped inside. Sunday shut the door and latched it. "Can't believe I'm doing this again."

Gabby took the knife out and flicked it open. Sunday reached over and collapsed it within a gentle fist. "You won't need that right now. Trip is a little bumpy. Don't want you to lose it."

Gabby nodded, stowing the pigsticker in her jacket. "Do we have to like, climb into the toilet or something?"

"Nah, they come to us." His leg burned like the handle on a skillet. He winced. "Should be here soon."

"Who is it? Who comes to get us?"

The unit rumbled. Gabby's knees buckled, but she caught herself.

"It's not a person really," said Sunday, casually taking hold of a handle as the unit jolted hard to one side eliciting a scream from Gabby. "It's more akin to like if a frog was a tarp and covered in claws and meat preservative."

"What's going on?"

"This is expected. *Regular default.*" A vibration emanated from deep below them. Then a monstrous sucking noise. "Here she comes."

The stalk emerged. Gabby emptied her lungs in a full-throated scream, then filled them once more and emptied them again. As its skin began to expand, Sunday dropped to the floor.

"It's easier if you assume the position."

Still shrieking, Gabby joined him, wrapping her hands around her knees.

The head of the stalk shot up and its skin engulfed the ceiling and walls. Having been through it before, Sunday was more able to contain his terror, allowing himself to be buffeted as the unit rocked. With a chance to rescue his mother, he was feeling very *Lemmy* about things. Meanwhile, the sound coming out of Gabriela seemed powered by an unlimited reserve. If anything, Sunday was impressed. He nudged her away from the wall as the spiked membrane crawled within inches of her skin. She returned this gesture with more screaming and an accusatory look for having undersold the horror of the moment. Colors in all wavelengths coursed the stalk. Holes opened, ejecting a foul, black-purple slurry over both passengers. Gabby took the brunt with her face, cutting off her shrieking. The smell was like a dumpster full of corpses cooking in the Texas sun. Sunday's stomach revolted, squelching hot bile into his throat. His mouth filled just as the skin snapped them up and swallowed them down.

Chapter Eighteen

A Curse for Cherries

They burst from the antique latrine and rolled across the pounded dirt of the Twilight Faire. Sunday bent over and blew out his corndog. Gabby's horror morphed into a stream of expletives as she wiped the slimy unguent from her eyes and gagged her tongue out. The stench was worse than Sunday remembered, like the unholy steam of mulled assholes in a crockpot.

"Yeah," he muttered, wiping himself down. "I tried a scuba suit last time, but it didn't help."

Gabby's eyes were like flashlights in the inky expanse of her face. She screamed again, right at him like a cooper's hawk with its toe stepped on.

"You get used to–"

Someone shoulder checked him. They shambled by with the skin of their arms hanging off. More followed, a steady stream of pallid strangers drawn toward violent entertainments. They moved specter-like, though the shuffling of their feet in the mud and straw betrayed their corporeal states. The Twilight Faire was open for business.

"Not good. Come on," snarled Sunday through gritted teeth.

Gabby scooched close, pressing her shoulder against Sunday's arm. There were all the rides and attractions as before, now up and running, and full of people. The *Mournful-Go-Round* spun slowly around a central hub. Riders were strapped into chairs and attached to their faces were what looked like long binoculars. They moaned and cried while they spun. Over at *Doom Bingo*, someone exclaimed that they'd won and the trouper working the game threw a rock at the winner's face. The line for the *Eurasian Freak Maze* stretched down the midway. The *Tilt-N-Hurl* was performing up to its name. So were the *Knife Dodge*, the *Gut Scrambler*, and the *Perpetual Wheel*. Sunday raced ahead as Gabby monologued her shock and disgust.

People flowed like drunken ants, their faces slack and slow to express. Their bodies moved in the same way, not exactly in sync but sapped of the energy of self-authored thought. Like a mass hypnosis. But beneath their zombied countenances, their eyes sparked with awareness. Sunday recognized surprise in those eyes at seeing he and Gabby moving against the current, but their mouths weren't capable of forming the questions in their minds.

Looking over the top of the crowd, as Sunday was taller than most, he saw the image from his visions. Bold stripes of the big top tent at the distant end of the midway. As in his original daydream, it was turning, the whole damned thing, like it had burrowed up from the depths of Hades. If there was a level deeper than the hell they currently occupied, well he didn't care much to see it.

They reached *The Skinner*. It was stopped as a new round of riders finished boarding. Faceless Roy was there at the controls, guiding them into the pill-shaped compartments at the end of each cephalopodian arm. With all on board, it began to turn as music played, a minor chord ditty hammered out by a sadist on an accordion. The arms traveled up and down until the passengers pleaded for it to stop. This was true even though it looked like they'd all boarded of their own free will. Moans and screams howled from within as the pods rotated, and not the noises a human makes from fear, but rather from active mutilation. The slicing holes which formed the metal skin of the compartments took their cut as the people tumbled within, and from those poured trembling strings of spaghettified flesh.

The ground within the circumference of the ride was a wet and bloody mass of grated skin, fat, and muscle. It steamed like dinner in the cold air of Cadogan's underworld.

"Roy!" called Sunday. He didn't know why. To test the man's awareness maybe. Or his own. To ask him why he did it. But the faceless teen only glanced his way, then back at the ride like an automaton.

"Sunday!" insisted Gabby. "Sunday!"

Gabby was surrounded by carnival goers. They stood close, eyeing her suspiciously. Their attention expanded to Sunday, a form of curiosity edged with malice. "Yeah, okay, let's go."

They broke through the scrum and advanced down the midway.

"Where are we going now?"

"*Un-house.* That's where my mom is. Keep your eye out for Ms. Poppy."

"I don't know what she looks like."

"She's a tiny old black lady. We'll probably hear her first. Talking shit wherever she is." He pushed through a line of people waiting in line for the *Splinter Oculus*, and to where the midway was crossed by another thoroughfare. Gabby struggled to stay close. Sunday glanced back. "Shouldn't you be trying to find Cadogan? Break your blood curse?"

"Uh, yeah. Sure, once I locate the *Ape of Sky.*"

"Reckon it's close to that," said Sunday, pointing to the big top tent which, now proximate, loomed large. "Probably inside."

"Yeah, okay," said Gabby, passing her pigsticker between hands.

Sunday angled toward the *Un-house*, noting that it had no people waiting to go in. "Good luck and whatnot."

"I would actually like your help with Cadogan."

Sunday glared.

She cleared her throat. "See, the thing is, I sort of maybe embellished some stuff. The blood curse bit is true, but the me having to do the killing ... I made that up so you'd have to take me." She smiled like a fox in a spotlight on the henhouse steps. "I mean, it *could* be true."

"You little idiot! You might end up getting killed!"

"I didn't make it all up! My family *is* cursed. I'm sorry I lied about—"

"Hold that thought," said Sunday, his face like a raptor on a rabbit at a thousand yards. "You see that? The dark beneath that trailer? Keep that pigsticker handy."

There was a shadowy space beneath the raised boards of an attraction called *Snakes!* and movement beneath. Something the size of the wild hogs that sometimes paraded through downtown Glen Rose like one of their own had just been elected mayor. One, two—no, three of them. Four! A face, a terrible face, emerged from the darkness. It belonged to a human child, except the nose was indeed a snout, all sniffing at the air and dripping wetness. It lumbered on hairy arms that were too short for the body, the fingers on the balled-up hands melded together with only a single cleft remaining near the center. A torn and mangled *Frozen 2* t-shirt hung from its over-muscled back.

Gabby gasped.

"That'll be the Doucets."

"Who?"

"Just some kids from the trailer park. I recon that's the girl one," he said, squinting.

"Those are kids?"

"Were. They're pork urchins now." The four hog children burst from the shadows at full gallop. Sunday drew Ms. Poppy's revolver and pulled the hammer. He posted up sideways, raised the gun and fired a shot over the charging swine, scattering them to the sides like cockroaches in an open drawer. "Now's good."

They pounded down the side alley for the *Un-house* as the Doucets rounded into the shadows. Halfway there, they charged out from behind. Sunday stopped shy of the trailer steps, took Gabby by the waist and tossed her up onto the walkway fronting the *Un-house* doors, and leveled the revolver once more. This time the pigs showed little fear, perhaps sensing that the man wasn't willing to do what he threatened, which was a fair read by them. Sunday had no love for the little buggers, but they were children of a sort, and he wanted nothing more than to return them alive to their parents as retribution for having made them. Gun brandished, Sunday backed toward the *Un-house* and swung himself onto the boards. The urchins ran to the stairs and oinked in frustration as they battled with the steps. Sunday pulled the big door open and Gabby slipped inside. A booger-faced Doucet leapt onto the boards just as Sunday slammed the door in its face.

"Will they get in?"

"I don't think they can reach the door handle and if they do, well I don't think their little fingers will get purchase, but no reason to stand around discussing it." He started through the opening hallway, past the gruesome photographs of marinating children and those already cooked.

Gabby was taking them in, muttering "Oh my God" over and over.

The mock kitchenette was still there when Sunday pushed through the door. In some ways it was the worst thing he'd seen at the Faire, part of his home reproduced as a prison for his mother. It was uncanny and manipulative. Did she create it or did Cadogan? And why?

"What is this place?" said Gabby.

"Don't know."

They entered the mirror maze, and it was here that Sunday stopped cold.

The glass was nearly black with ink. So full of his mother's writing that only tiny glimmers of mirror shined back.

"Whoa."

Sunday felt thickness in his throat, swallowed it away then headed in. As the walls were no longer mirrored, the path through the maze was easily blazed.

Gabby lagged, trying to make sense of the writing. "What is all this?"

"Mom thinks this place is giving her memories back so she's writing them down so she doesn't lose them."

"Why?"

"She's got dementia."

"I don't think this is her handwriting."

Sunday stopped in the dim corridor and stomped back to Gabby, finger jabbed to a sentence on the wall. "That's her handwriting, a little more manic than usual, but that's all her. How do you know her handwriting?"

"Well, what I mean is, there's no way this is her story. See?" She pointed to a line. "She wasn't born in 1889 near Ballyheigue, Ireland, was she?"

"No," said Sunday, still scanning. "She fucking wasn't."

...AND THE LAND SO WET THAT NOTHING BUT GRASSES
WOULD GROW. LIKE EVERY OTHER FAMILY IN COUNTY
KERRY, YOURS RESTED UPON THE BACK OF THE COWS
YOUR FATHER PURCHASED AND RAISED. SO WENT THE
COWS, SO WENT THE FAMILY. WHEN THREE OF THE FAMI—
LY'S FIVE COWS TOOK ILL AND HAD TO BE PUT DOWN, IT WAS
HARD TIMES. FATHER LEFT IN SEARCH OF WORK, LEAVING
YOU AND MA AND THE LITTLE ONES. YOU LOOKED FOR
WORK TOO BUT NONE COULD BE FOUND. ONE DAY, WHILE
OUT WANDERING, YOU CAME ACROSS AN ORCHARD ON A
LANE. CHERRY TREES DROOPING WITH FRUIT. BUT YOU'D
NEVER SEEN AN ORCHARD AND YOU TOOK TO STEALING
THE CHERRIES YOU FOUND THERE.

"This is straight from his diaries!" Gabby exclaimed. "I mean, not exactly,
but it's the same story he wrote there. I know how it goes! He starts
stealing the cherries and bringing them home. He travels out at night
with a basket and fills it. The family eats. They sell cherry breads for
money. But then one night the owner of the orchard is waiting for him.
A witch." Gabby scooted down the mirrors, looking for the reference.
"Here!"

YOU GOT GREEDY, ACANTHUS, YOU WENT TOO OFTEN, STOLE
TOO MUCH. AND THE ORCHARD'S OWNER SOON WAITED
FOR YOU. SOME BECLOAKED PERSON. FACE OBSCURED
BENEATH HOOD, BUT WHO SPOKE WITH THE VOICE OF A
WOMAN. "MY CHILD, I INVITE YOU TO STAY," SHE SAID. WHEN
YOU TRIED TO RUN, YOU FOUND THAT YOUR FEET WOULD
NOT CARRY YOU BEYOND THE OUTER ROWS OF TREES,
AND THUS YOU BECAME IMPRISONED.

"See? I told you! That's the curse! Same as my family's."

Sunday's voice was gravel. "Why is my mom writing Cadogan's biography?"

"I don't know." She skipped down a few panels of glass, running her fingers over the writing.

"Let's go."

"Hold on, hold on. Right here." She thumped the mirror. "Come on, read it."

Sunday leaned in.

IT WAS FIVE YEARS YOU LIVED WITH THE WITCH. NEVER SEEING HER FACE. NEVER LEARNING HER NAME. NEVER SEEING YOUR FAMILY, NOT KNOWING THEIR FATES. ONE NIGHT, WHEN SHE CAME TO YOUR ROOM WITH MILK AND CHERRIES, AND LAID HER LIPS UPON YOUR FOREHEAD, YOU PUT THE SHARPENED END OF A LIMB INTO HER HEART.

SHE CAME TO REST UPON YOU, BASTING YOU IN HER BLOOD, HER POWER. WASTING NO TIME, YOU RAN AND FOUND THAT YOU COULD BREAK THE LINE OF TREES AT THE ORCHARD'S EDGE AND THAT THE CURSE THE WITCH HAD UPON YOU WAS BROKE. YOU RAN UNTIL YOU REACHED HOME. AND THERE YOU FOUND YOUR MOTHER AND THREE YOUNGER SIBLINGS LONG ROTTED IN THE CORNER OF THE ROOM, STARVED TO DEATH. THE AIR NO LONGER REEKED OF DECAY, ONLY THE AROMA OF PULPED CHERRIES.

Sunday moved ahead, saying nothing. Why was Cadogan using his mother to record his life story onto funhouse mirrors? He felt a new urgency as they traveled through the maze. Something that nagged at him. An impending sense of doom. The loss of his mother.

He was nearly running now, with Gabby's shoes squeaking trying to match his pace. Several times, they retreated from dead ends. Then came a familiar set of turns and finally the long hallway. There Sunday stopped waiting to see if his mother appeared. His nose caught a whiff of her hair, her lavender shampoo. Then a voice came behind.

"I'm ready."

Chapter Nineteen
The Spindle

Regina McWhorter stood naked, shining red as a roman candle with a uranium smile. "Hello Sunday. Hello Gabriela."

"How do you know my name?"

Sunday rushed to her, reached into the cargo hold of his coveralls and unspooled a dress like a magician's scarf. Remembering his mother's bare state, he'd brought along one of her favorite sun dresses.

"There's no need for that, baby," she said, though she offered no resistance when he pulled the garment over her head. "We're all naked beneath."

"Can't have you jumping back to Dublin in your birthday suit, Mom."

Regina grinned at Gabby as Sunday straightened the dress over her tired flesh. "You. I know you. You're somebody special. Somebody *important.*"

"What's that supposed to mean?"

"Young woman. You are blood. Borne of this beautiful place." She held her arms out and bowed as if beholding the matriarch of a royal family.

"The heck are you talking about?"

Regina smiled wide.

"Sorry, I didn't think to bring shoes," said Sunday, still tending to his mom.

Regina pointed a knobby finger at Gabby. "You're the one."

Gabby shook her head and opened the pouch for the pocket watch. "Sunday! Look! It's down to two o'clock! How is that possible? How long have we been here?"

"Dunno. We're not in a real place."

"Not *yet*," said Regina, eyes sparkling and keen upon the pocket watch. "Ooooo, now where did you find that?"

"Always had it," said Gabby.

Sunday took Regina by the hand. "Come on." She blithely followed, offering no resistance other than a stuttering gait.

Gabby darted toward the entrance of the *Un-house*, following a single, long finger smudge she'd left through the writing. Sunday pulled Regina by the sleeve of her dress, furious at her lack of urgency. "Mom, can you hop to it?" He did a double take, eyes drawn to her red skin. "What is that, anyway? Paint?"

Regina loosely considered herself. "Paint? I don't know. Feels like … marinade."

"The damned hell what?"

They made their way through the mockup of Sunday's trailer, then into the front hallway and to the big doors. Gabby spun around as if to block it. "The Doucets!"

Regina laughed. "Those kids! Managed to follow us through the realms, didn't they?" She gestured Gabby aside. "They won't hurt you. Come." She led the way, pushing the doors open to the glare of flashing lights, the cacophony of organ grinding, the din of rides and attractions, the ever-swelling crowd. The Doucets were nowhere in sight.

"Where are all these people coming from?" said Gabby.

"All around. They're coming for the celebration," Regina said.

They descended the stairs and pushed through the throng. Faces stared, irritated and fuming at the intruders with their captive. At the midway, Sunday pulled Regina in the direction of the portal and found sudden, impossible resistance. "Ma! Let's go!"

"Hey!" said Gabby, edging in the direction of the big top. "We're all gonna be trapped here if the countdown finishes. Help me with Cadogan."

Sunday hardly heard it. In the moment he cared only about protecting his mother, fulfilling his promise, his duty to keep her safe. His own voice rang in his ears: *get her back, get her back, get her back.* She allowed him to pull on her arm but was unmoved by his efforts. "I told you, I don't want to go. All will be lost. Here, I know my life. My journey. I don't forget anymore. And besides, I couldn't leave if I wanted to now, which I don't."

"What are you talking about?"

"All of my memories have been returned. In exchange, I will serve as vessel."

"You're talking about the writing! He's been filling your mind with his own history."

"My mind is home to my life and soon to his."

"Cadogan's inside you?"

Her eyes sparkled like a welding torch. "Not yet."

Sunday tugged her arm again but feared injury. Regina was implacable. Tears gathered on the surface of his eyes. "You said you were ready to go home."

"I said no such thing, child. I said I was *ready*."

"Sunday!" cried Gabby, holding up the watch, its little hands moving faster. "I'm going."

He released his mom, who glanced to the big top, which had grown to its full height, towering over the Faire. "I wish you would come with me. To stand by my side upon the joining of spirits."

"He's in the big tent, isn't he?"

"Where he's been since the return." She took his hand and guided him to the midway as the sea of people parted before them. Gabby galloped ahead.

Sunday felt small and weak. Like a child. Once again helpless to divert his mother's destiny.

He allowed himself to be led along, eyes down, weary of seeing anything more of the Twilight Faire than the pummeled dirt and hay of its ground. He could hear it though. The movement of rides grinding in perpetuity, the howls of those bidden to come aboard as they experienced some novel torture to expand the boundaries of their suffering. He smelled the intermingling of mystery meat boiled in rancid frying grease with the aroma of stress and fear, felt his stomach boil hot into his gullet. Still, he watched the ground. Giving witness in addition to every other sense might break his mind.

"Come one, come all! Test your belief in the Whip of Faith!"

Sunday halted in his tracks and scanned the grounds. When the call came again, he zeroed in on a smallish ride just beyond the first line of larger attractions. It was a simple setup, a wagon wheel lit with bright yellows and reds, and people strapped to the spokes. He made a beeline. Regina followed, unbothered by the detour.

Sunday dashed under the flashing sign for the *Whip of Faith* and to a tiny woman standing atop a steep set of metal stairs. "Ms. Poppy!"

At first, she didn't seem to hear him, but then she stopped her crowd work and angled her head slowly down. Her eyes were wide and bloodshot in an emaciated face, and framed by hair, wild and filthy. Syrupy pink tears streamed down her cheeks and off her chin. A long, foul-smelling cigar poked out from her teeth. The hint of a smile bumped upon her countenance, then disappeared.

"Hello."

Sunday started up the stairs.

"What are you doing?" asked Regina.

"I'm getting Ms. Poppy. What's it look like?"

"She belongs here now. She's willing to stay. To be my friend forever." She flashed her yellow grin. "Aren't you, Poppy?"

Ms. Poppy was paralyzed by Regina's gaze, her face gerning into a contradictory tangle of expressions before resolving to a flat affect. "Yes, that's it," she said. "Friend."

"See? More loyalty even than from my own son."

"Come on, Ms. Poppy. Let's go," Sunday said, reaching for her.

"No," she said, stepping back. "I want to stay here." She turned to a panel of rusty controls and yanked on a lever. The wheel upon which people were strapped began to spin and they started to scream. "The Whip of Faith is a test of belief in oneself," she said to no one in particular.

The wheel spun faster and faster. The riders' arms flopped out from their sides, pulled by the centrifugal force above their heads, making them look like sun worshippers affixed to a turbocharged pinwheel.

Their screams formed an echoing chorus like the howl of a train in a tunnel, then slowly died away as they lost consciousness one-by-one. Sunday expected Ms. Poppy to shut down the machine. She pushed the lever to the side and with an earsplitting whine, the machine sped up. Sleeping faces darkened red to purple to plum, swelling, distorting, engorging with blood.

"You gotta stop that now, Ms. Poppy. These folks are gonna die."

She blew out a long serpent of smoke. "You can't die here."

Sunday felt something on his shoulder, his mother's hand.

"You can only suffer," she whispered.

The faces were a blur, a ring of purple at the circumference of the wheel. Then the wheel gained contrast as it was set against a red shadow Sunday knew was the air filling with a mist of blood oozing from eyes, ears, noses, and mouths of the riders. One of the faces unraveled completely, a wet rag of degloved skin tossed like a sock. Then every face pulled free and went flying out from the wheel like cake batter on a blender beater. Sunday had enough of discarded faces. He spun around and marched through the crowd into the midway. He had to find Gabby. He had to end this.

Regina caught up quickly. "What's the matter, baby?"

"Why you'd want to be the queen of this place? I can't understand! The torture? The suffering? It's just hell with funnel cake."

"Oh, that's not true. *Not* true." She came alongside and threw her arms out. "Hell may or not be real, I don't much know. And yes, there is suffering here. But it serves a purpose."

"I know all about it. Punish the sinners," he said, picking up the pace to the big top.

"No! Suffering as punishment is the stupidest idea I've ever heard of. It's meaningless and wasteful. What Acanthus understands is that nothing is more real than suffering. Entire universes exist in a single moment of undistilled suffering. It's the fiber we spin to build a tangible weft between the imagined and the physical. We use it to pull the two into one. These attractions, these rides and machines … they aren't here for entertainment. Each one is its own chamber, a carefully designed tool for extracting unadulterated, undistilled *reality*."

"Reality being suffering."

Sunday pushed past a ghoulish old man with his head split in two.

"That's about the measure of it, yes. Think of the Twilight Faire as suspended right up against the membrane of the world's underbelly. Extract enough suffering, spin enough thread and you have a rope to the physical world. Then it's just a matter of pulling the two together," she said, clapping her hands.

"And you're fine just letting all these people suffer to make this place *real*. Letting Ms. Poppy suffer?" He shook his head. *This wasn't his mother.* "No. You're not yourself. He's poisoned you. You'd never let this happen. You're just deluded."

"I'm the opposite of deluded. I am a lens of clarity."

"This is some kind of nightmare. You can't manifest something in the physical world just by making people suffer."

"That's quite a true point. There's one more necessary ingredient needed to show the threads where to coalesce, something upon which to weave the rope of reality together."

"Oh yeah? What's that? *You?* Are you supposed to be the ingredient?"

"No, no. You're not listening. I'm the vessel, not the spindle!"

"Spindle?"

"That which connects the ascending spirit to the physical world. Something once possessed on both sides of the membrane. No one we have yet summoned to the Faire has brought with them such an item. We've been waiting patiently. But that wait has ended."

Sunday angrily pushed a lumbering faire-goer out of the way. "Move!" He glared back at his mother, following casually, gait steady but crooked. "What do you mean? I haven't seen any spindle."

"It's a metaphor, baby."

"Okay but what is it? Possessed on both sides of the membrane? What—" Sunday felt his heart thump. "The watch."

A smile like a mouth full of lemon peel.

"The watch."

Chapter Twenty
Monkey Business

S unday had never run so hard in all his life, even harder than the first
time the Doucets tried to eat him. Gabby had gone off to confront
her distant relation and resolve an arcane blood curse while unknowingly
delivering the key that would unleash all unbridled fuck. He had to
retrieve the pocket watch before A.V. Cadogan knew she had it. Or did
he already?

Good goddamned, he was out of shape.

The big top loomed. Sunday's breath wheezed through his throat like
a whistle half plugged with phlegm. He tried to ignore his mother, now
floating beside him via some dark force of levitation. The stitch in his
side was like a jumper cable clamped to his love handle. He lunged ahead.
"Outta my way!"

"Excuse us. This is my son, Sunday. He's normally not so rude,"
Regina assured the crowd in a placating tone.

The attendees nodded vague understanding, grunted, and cleared the
way.

Sunday stumbled to the thick outer skin of the tent. He leaned on one of the huge wooden poles while catching his breath.

"Gabby."

"Oh, she's in here," Regina said, motioning to the tent flap. It opened by itself, pulling wide.

The inside of the tent was like an optical illusion, appearing many times the size of its gigantic outer profile. They stood along the top row of benches, looking down, so far down, toward the floor where three huge rings were set amid rigging and towers for trapeze artists and Lemmy knows what else. Sunday's heaving breath went short. Smack in the middle of the center ring stood a forty-foot high honest-to-goodness primate simian. *The Ape of Sky* Gabby told him about. Its fur had grown back. *Where was she?*

People filtered in from points along the perimeter, taking to the bleachers with boxes of rancid peanuts and waxy cups filled to the brim with stagnant toilet water. Sunday caught a whiff and retched.

"They're here for you and me," said Regina, giving his hand a squeeze. "I want you to meet Acanthus Vervain Cadogan. Your new father."

"The fuck he is."

"Sunday," she said, bottom lip pushed out like a child losing their dessert privileges.

"I got no use for a father. And you don't need a new husband."

Regina shook her head. "Oh, I'm not getting married, baby."

They made their way down the long aisle toward the dirt floor under the monkey's gaze. Sunday scanned the faces for Gabby.

"So, where is he?" Sunday demanded, pulling his hand away. "Where's this great man who gave you your memories back?"

"He's everywhere," Regina replied, winking as if they now shared a secret.

"Jesus Christ."

"*No, not him.*"

They reached the bottom, falling into the shadow cast by the strangely proportioned mechanical primate. Sunday scanned the stands, which were now suddenly full and extending further than the distance they'd traversed.

"Where's Gabby, mom?"

Regina grinned as shadows began to move. Sunday met the yellow eyes of *The Ape of Sky* looking down. He felt a shudder in his chest but then remembered that Gabby had said the thing was animatronic. Like Big Tex at the State Fair. Of course, Big Tex had never *looked* at him, much less addressed him personally.

"Hello, Sunday," said the monkey in a voice like the core of the earth learning to speak. "I'm so happy you've joined us."

"The fuck I have, Cadogan. Come on out of there, why don't you?"

The monkey slowly moved its head side to side, the muffled sound of whirring motors and gears churning.

Regina floated up. "He's not bodily right now."

"Not bodily?" Sunday tilted his head and searched her face for any sign of his mom.

More mechanical buzzing and clunking from inside the giant chimp-mech. "Your mother has generously offered herself to me, to share her mind. But only if I convinced you to stay with her, here. Voluntarily."

"Well, then, no." Sunday spun around and started walking. "Come on mom."

"So quick to decide," said the voice, gaining flesh, less metallic. "I always savored a negotiation. How's this: I'll free Ms. Poppy if you stay. Does that sound appetizing?"

"How the fuck is a hostage situation voluntary?"

"It presents a choice, does it not?"

"Free my friend and lose my mother or get my mom back and lose my friend."

The huge ape lowered its head far enough it could have swallowed him. The eyes darkened from yellow to purple to deep red.

"You're losing her, anyway."

He turned to Regina. "Mom. Come home."

"I don't want to disappear."

He took her by the shoulders, studying her to find a way in.

"Stay with me," she said. "I love you."

"I wonder if you do, Mom."

"How *dare* you," she growled, her teeth flashed sharp and radiant.

"Think about our home. We live together. We're pretty happy. I cook us breakfast every day. The yolks are never broken and we always have Cholula. You've got your flower garden. Can you remember that?" His voice trembled. "You have little daisies and coneflowers and beebalm, and these hot pink knockout roses. That garden is your favorite thing."

"I can have a garden here."

"This place isn't about you, it's about him! Cadogan is using you, can't you see that?"

"It's a trade. We both get something."

Sunday wrapped his arms around her, squeezing, trying to make her remember their bond, only to find her rigid and wooden, cold.

"Please, please, please," he cried into her neck, conscious of his tears wetting her hair. "I need you. I need you with me. We all need you. This place will kill you. Mom, please!"

Then pain, sudden sharp pain in his arms and hands. Flinching away, he watched blood trickle from dozens of holes his palms and forearms. Her skin had sprouted the long, slender thorns of a huisache tree.

Sorrow filled his chest like a river under flood, crowding out the pain. It was over. She was never coming back.

Regina opened her needled arms. "Stay with me."

Sunday gulped a breath and simply whispered, "No ... no."

"You must, my baby boy. My Prince of the Twilight Faire!"

He shook his head. "I'm done fighting with you. If you want to stay here, I guess that's your decision. But don't make me part of a hostage trade. Let Ms. Poppy go. Let us go."

The air took on the smell of burning hair.

The Ape of Sky moved and Sunday danced away. It leaned back, going from a crawling position to a seat, shaking the ground.

"I have freed Ms. Poppy as a showing of my good faith," it said. "Of course, it won't matter soon. When the Twilight Faire ascends, you'll all be right back on the midway enjoying the rides. Along with everyone else on Earth."

The Ape was backlit by twinkling lights and a thick, yellow haze, putrid like a knocked over port-o-let simmering on August asphalt.

"What's that smell?" he wondered aloud.

Gabby came roaring around from the monkey's backside at a full clip, wielding a flaming acrobat's baton. She shot past and skid to a halt.

"Let's go!"

"What'd you do?"

"He's in the monkey!"

Flames licked up the ape's backside and Sunday realized the crazy teen had lit her double-great-grandpa on fire. It was a bold move by any standard and had to piss him off considering his history of immolation.

Gabby opened the pocket watch. "Ten minutes left! We gotta go!"

The flaming monkey lurched forward, its face a horrible, sharp-toothed grimace backlit by fire. "My watch!" it growled.

"Keep it!" yelled Gabby, hurling it at the ape.

Sunday snatched it from the air. "Nope!" he exclaimed, surprised by his dexterity.

Regina came close. "Give it to me. I need it."

Ass on fire, *The Ape of Sky* lurched from its foundations and stalked ponderously toward them.

"You need this?" said Sunday, taunting with the watch. "You want this?"

Regina eyes dazzled at the sight of the watch, as if trapped by its spell. "I do, we do. It's the only way."

Sunday shot up the aisle toward the exit. "Let's go, Gabby!"

"What are we doing?"

"Getting home!"

Behind, Regina shambled off balance, pleading for them to come back, then screaming. The Ape, engulfed in flame, pounded forward. It wobbled after them, the electronic works within exposed as the skin scorched away. Pistons and gears popped and whirled amid gobs of pink, plasticine gunk. Sunday shot a glance at Gabby. "What'd you do?"

"Shoved about two pounds of Laffy Taffy up its ass!"

Tangled cables melted as the flaming Ape seized to a halt. It teetered off balance and fell forward, clawed arms pinned beneath its chest. The crowd roared and clapped at the bonus feature they'd been treated to.

They neared the top of the aisle where the tent flap opened onto the midway. *The Ape of Sky*—Cadogan—crashed down. The blood-glow eyes flickered and died. The tent fell silent as the motors whined to a stop.

"Ha ha! Yes! Suck it!" Gabby cried.

Sunday turned to his mother, stumbling up to them. "Let's go."

Regina stood in the aisle, a brittle smile scything across her face.

"Mom?"

One of her eyes blinked red, then the other, alternating rapidly until both glowed just as the Ape's had.

"Shit," said Gabby.

"Ma?"

Her voice was two voices now, a disharmonious chord.

"I need that watch, baby."

"I'm not *your* baby. And you sure as shit ain't my mom." He pushed Gabby ahead. "Run!"

Regina's mouth opened bullhorn wide, shining bright like a circus spotlight. The sound that came out of it rippled the walls of the tent.

"THE SPINDLE!"

Sunday shot through the flap after Gabby. "Come and get it!"

Chapter
Twenty-One

Shitshow

G abby's youthful stride outpaced Sunday. He did his best to keep up but age and a diet of mostly Shiner Bock hampered his athleticism. Regina, or whatever she was now, levitated above the crowd, mouth open and shining. Gabby stretched the distance. Sunday cried out and she slowed. He stumbled up to her.

"You're faster. Take the watch."

Gabby took it. Sunday pointed into the distance. "Find that port-a-john and get the fuck outa here. I'll try to hold them off. They still think I've got it." Gabby nodded and gave him one of those looks that people get when they're definitely going to die in a movie. She disappeared into the crowd.

Regina flew closer. Sunday ducked beneath the awning of a carnival game called the E-LIMB-INATOR as her spotlight flashed by. He backed up to the counter. A deafening blast went off right next to him.

The game was a version of the classic target-shooting carnival game. Only instead of water guns or rubber band pistols, E-LIMB-INA-TOR contestants wielded double barrel pump-action shotguns. Twelve gauges. Their blindfolded targets, fellow Faire attendees, rumbled by on conveyor belts, squirming against bindings and ball gags. Many were missing hands, feet, or entire limbs. One man, still alive of course, had been blown clean in half, with his legs and gut-dripping torso traveling on the belts in opposite directions. Sunday winced at the brutality of Cadogan's creation.

He summoned the attendant, a teen with awful posture and a missing ear. "Hey there buddy, how many shells in these?"

"Five per barrel, but they're only for—"

"That's great."

Sunday snatched one of the shotguns. He took a step, reconsidered, and grabbed a second one before turning to go.

"Hey! Those are for players only!"

Sunday charged into the midway with a shotgun on each arm. He spotted his mom in the distance, heading toward the portal and pulled both triggers to get her attention. *Ba-boom.* "Hey Mom!" he cried. "Come get me! I want to stay!" Then he bumbled across the thorough-fare toward *Doom Bingo* and the *Gut Scrambler*, firing again.

The knit of the crowd tightened.

"Move! Go on now, git!"

They stiffened, refusing to give clear passage.

"Don't make me open up on y'all."

Regina's yellow light appeared overhead like a miniature sun. She'd doubled back and was hovering toward him. Good for Gabby, bad for Sunday. He broke away and ran in the opposite direction. He had no plan other than to put distance between his mother and the watch.

Maybe he was destined to spend eternity down here with her. With them. Maybe that was the cost of keeping the place from becoming real.

She flew overhead, delivering a mother's words in her new voice. Sunday refused to engage, just kept running. The ground vibrated beneath his feet just as a heavy rumbling sounded from the direction he was headed. Was it *The Ape of Sky*, magically recovered and coming to finish him off? Regina's face had gone sour. Up ahead, bodies rag-dolled through the air, launched upward like they'd been through a snowblower. The crowd dispersed. Regina veered sideways at the last moment.

It was just about the biggest tractor he'd ever seen. And with Ms. Poppy driving it. The steering wheel was so big, she was like a diminutive ship's captain trying to wrangle the helm. She tossed the cigar from her mouth and hollered, "Grab on!"

He skidded to a stop, then turned to run alongside. Abandoning one of the shotguns to take hold of a handle, he hopped onto the running board. The crowd clambered after him, but a dose of buckshot cleared the way.

"Didn't know you could operate a tractor," he said, hooking his elbow onto the chrome handle and pumping the shotty.

"No harder than my Rascal. More fun. Might get one of these when we get home. Tell me Sunday, how do we do that?"

He pointed down the midway. "Keep going that way!"

Regina dropped out of the sky and came at them headlong. Ms. Poppy was nonchalant. "Your mom's flying."

"That's not her anymore. She's Cadogan."

Regina slammed onto the hood of the tractor, hands and feet gripping the steel like talons.

"Give me the Spindle!" she roared. "OBEY!"

"Give her the Spindle!"

"Nope!"

Regina scurried like a beetle over the body of the tractor and down to where Sunday held on.

"Shoot her! She's not your mom anymore!"

Ms. Poppy was right. Summoning his resolve, he lowered the barrel to her face. Her hair whipped wildly in the wind and all he could think about was looking for a scrunchie so he could tie it up for her.

She ripped away the shotgun and hurled it across the Faire, then slapped at his clothes, searching. "Give it to me."

Something in his face must have betrayed the truth.

She gripped his shirt and pulled him close, glowing teeth bared. "Where is it?"

He shook his head.

She shoved him away and squinted, searching his eyes. "Ah."

She leapt into the sky, then coursed down the midway.

"Where's she going?"

Sunday secured his grip. "Faster, Ms. Poppy. She's going after Gabby."

The tractor's motor roared. Black smoke billowed from the stacks.

The crowd had cleared to the sides. In the distance was Gabby, running toward the old outhouse. The Doucets were in pursuit, followed by Regina.

The tractor rolled up on them fast. Sunday leapt from the sideboard, his overworked ankles and quivering calf muscles nearing the limits of their endurance. Fifty feet from the shitter, an urchin jumped onto Gabby's back, dragging her to the ground like a lion taking down a gazelle. Another took hold of her arm.

Regina settled onto the dirt, smiling and calm. Sunday booted a Doucet from where it had Gabby by the foot. It tumbled away like a sausage on a warped skillet.

Another Doucet swallowed Gabby's entire hand in its toothy mouth. Fighting through the pain, she cried out, "I can't hold on!"

The urchin would chew her hand off to get the pocket watch. Sunday latched onto the piggy's rotund little body.

"Gabby, let go of it!"

"What? No!"

"Let go of the goddamned watch!"

She pulled her hand free of the jaws as Sunday hoisted the beast into his arms. It wriggled and squealed as he wrangled it, legs scrambling, teeth snapping.

"Little shit," he grunted, bear-hugging it like a keg of Shiner all the way to the outhouse.

Somewhere behind, Cadogan's voice boomed from his mother's vocal cords.

"GIVE ME THE SPINDLE!"

He reached the latrine with the swine and toed open the door. His leg went hot. As if it had been waiting for him, the slime-coated membrane crawled up from the toilet hole and ran over the surfaces. Sunday wrestled the shrieking Doucet inside and slammed it headfirst into the shitter. It struggled against the opening, then with a loud *THWOK*, was sucked inside.

The door hit him from behind as his mother slammed into it.

The membrane snapped closed and pulled him down.

Chapter
Twenty-Two
Backflow

S unday emerged from the yellow port-o-john like a frank squeezed out of a corny dog. Flopping around on the floor was the girl Doucet, filthy, but no longer ungulate. She looked up at him, confused but hostile.

"Which one are you?"

"Holly," she said, then spat in his face.

The portable rumbled. Sunday kicked open the door to the dawn beyond. "Out."

Holly Doucet got clear and Sunday hopped away. Slime geysered from the expanding toilet hole, which birthed, in order, Regina, Gabby, and Ms. Poppy.

Regina stumbled forward, dripping in muck. "Bay-bee," she said, her voice stretching and heavy like bread dough. "I need ... I need the Spindle. Give me..." her eyes fluttered and she slumped to the ground. "The watch ... the Spindle."

Sunday scooted closer, his hands out in a defensive posture. "Mom? I don't have it. I love you, but I wouldn't give it to you even if I did."

The reds of her eyes glistened and strobed, then one blinked back to normal, followed by the other. She coughed, cleared her throat, and gazed upon him clear-eyed.

"Sunday?"

He swallowed her into his embrace.

"Is that you? Is he gone?"

"I ... I don't know." She placed a hand over her stomach. "I don't feel great."

"Hell, none of us feel great."

He beamed at Gabby and Ms. Poppy.

"What now?" said Ms. Poppy, clearing a thick layer of purple ooze from her eyes.

Regina lurched out of Sunday's embrace and gagged out a string of black phlegm. He rubbed her back as she coughed, his eyes widening as the gunk became long and thick.

"What is that?" cried Gabby.

Regina crawled in fits and starts across the grass like a cat trying to regurgitate a hairball.

Sunday cried out, "Someone call 9-1-1!"

Regina stumbled forward, unable to get a steady knee under her body. Hunched over, she took hold of the inky rope and yanked it free of her throat like pulling a rat snake from a gopher hole. Then she was doubled over on all fours, arching her back. Her mouth stretched wide. Sunday got down on his knees, but didn't know what to do or how to comfort her. She seemed in the active throes of metamorphosis.

Something new breeched her lips. A tight bundle of thin, stick-like legs pushed stiffly out from her throat, their tiny ends shaking and tentative, stroking the air for purchase.

They emerged from Regina's tortured mouth, spreading wide in their journey to the ground and bending along segments. Eight of them. An egg-sized body came last, the color of oatmeal, and released itself from his mother. Sunday dragged her away.

"A spider!" cried Ms. Poppy.

"A Harvestman!" yelled Sunday, his skin crawling at the sight of the colossal daddy longlegs.

The arachnid was the size of a lawnmower. It spun in the dry grass of Dublin City Park and hissed through a pair of fangs.

"Daddy longlegs don't have teeth! Or wear goggles! That one's wearing goggles!"

Ms. Poppy was right. The damned Harvestman had goggles on.

"It's Acanthus," said Holly, laying in the grass munching a dandelion. "He's in the spider."

It sped around the group, skittering fast for the old portable.

Regina cried out, "Don't let him get back!"

It darted for the latrine. Sunday wheeled around to kick it but whiffed and fell on his ass. The spider leapt for the toilet, but the old portable hammered down before it could get inside. There was a loud pop and a squelch, the sound of Cadogan's spider guts boiling out. A few skinny legs twitched from beneath the portable until going still.

"Ha!" Gabby slapped her hands together from the opposite side of the fallen unit. "Got him. Blood curse broken."

Ms. Poppy rubbed her forehead. "I need Fireball. Somebody get me Fireball."

Regina sat on the ground, legs crossed. Sunday embraced her. "Is that it? Is he gone?"

"Yes. I think so," she sobbed.

"You're safe now."

She pushed away. Her eyes were raw and wet. "Please let go."

He released her shoulders. "But—"

She shook her head and looked away. "I told you what would happen. I'll lose it all again. Staying here is … it's death."

"What are you say—"

"Cadogan gave me my story back."

"He was using your body to bring himself back! Your mind!"

"And he's gone now," she said, and made eye contact with him, then Gabby and Ms. Poppy. "I don't feel him in my mind anymore. You all made us safe from him. You made me safe from him. But the only way I can hold onto my mind is to go back."

"How do you know the Twilight Faire didn't die with him?"

"It's real. It may not be here, but it didn't live in his imagination. It's free of his grip. It's adrift now. I can remake it. Shape it to my own vision. Into something beautiful and happy. It will take some time, some work."

"And what about all those people down there?" asked Gabby.

Regina sighed. "I don't know for sure, but I think they can go anytime they want. They're probably figuring that out right now."

Sunday eyed the portable, half expecting the teen Roy West Carpenter to come stumbling out.

Holly gagged.

"Nuh-uh. Not more of this bullshit," Ms. Poppy said.

Holly Doucet bent at the waist and vomited. Unperturbed, she cleared her throat and grabbed a stick, using it to fish the watch out from the pile of sick. Then she walked it over to Gabby and gave her the stick with the watch dangling at the end.

Regina took Sunday by the shoulders. "I have to go back, baby."

"I know," he said, surprising himself. "I know."

He took her by the hand. "I'll take you."

"No."

"I *have* to take you back. I've got the relic."

Regina looked at his leg. "I don't think you do."

Where the cooked rabbit eel had once been was now a deep, white scar spiraling up his leg.

"Well, shit."

Gabby cleared her throat. "It's okay. I think this will work." She wiped the sodden pocket watch in the grass. "This has got more magic juice in it than your leg thing, anyway." She offered it to Regina.

"Thank you, Gabriela." Regina pressed her fingers to the side of her head. "It starts like a migraine. I've got to go now before everything's lost."

The lump in Sunday's throat wouldn't swallow and all the sadness and stress and worry tried to gush out of his eyes, but he held it.

"Will you find some way to let me know you're okay? Send me a sign or something?"

"I will," she said, smiling brighter, and more genuinely, than she had in months. "I assume I can come up the pipes anytime I want."

Holly, with green on her teeth and petals on her lips said, "Will you send my brothers back?"

"After I teach them a thing or two about manners."

"You can try."

Regina wrapped her arms around her son as Gabby and Ms. Poppy got the old yellow latrine upright and Cadogan's remains scraped off. Every instinct Sunday had told him never to let her go. A good son wouldn't allow his mother to return to the hell they'd just escaped, no matter the reason.

"Sunday," Regina whispered.

He squeezed her tighter.

"The only way I get to keep you, is to let you go. And it's the only way you'll remember me whole."

Sunday pushed his nose into her neck, stroked her hair a final time. A memory kindled then, vivid. Of being a little boy and embracing her the same way when he had to go off to school for the first time. It must have been kindergarten. Until that point, they'd never been apart. Even when she worked, she'd always taken him with her. He still remembered what she'd whispered in his ear then: *if you can think of me, then we are together*. Letting her go now wasn't just the only way he'd remember her whole, it was the only way she'd remember him at all—the only way they could be together, even if they never saw each other again. "I know," he croaked at last.

"That's it, baby." She eased him away and held his gaze. "You'll water my garden?"

He nodded, knowing if he said anything more he'd melt into a puddle.

Gabby held the toilet open and nodded goodbye as Regina stepped inside. She turned to face them as the door closed. The latrine rumbled and Sunday knew she was gone.

The sky was blue and the sun was out. Sunday searched to the horizon and didn't see the faintest hint of purple.

They walked to Ms. Poppy's Firebird parked where they'd left it under the copse of trees at Dublin City Park. Sunday offered the car keys. "You want to drive or me?"

"Just get me home. I want to get as drunk as possible as quickly as possible." She kicked Holly out of the passenger seat. "Get in back, you little toilet gerbil."

Gabby joined the Doucet in the back seat.

Heading down the road, Sunday shouted over his shoulder. "Drop you at the shop?"

Wind lashed Gabby's hair. "Yep."

They pulled up to the Dublin Historical Showroom and Guided Audio Tour. Gabby got out and stood on the sidewalk. "That was weird."

"Well, yeah," said Sunday. "You alright? How's that hand?"

Gabby considered it. The wounds from Holly's attack while in her urchin-form had already begun to heal. "Seems like I'll be okay."

"Yeah. Injuries from down there seem to clear up pretty quick if you make it back."

"Guess so."

"Gonna tell your dad what happened?"

Gabby looked up and down the street and inhaled clean air. "No, I think I'm gonna steal his car and drive it to Marfa. Always wanted to go to Marfa. If the curse is lifted, I'll get there and I can give him the good news when I get back."

"Little civil disobedience to prove your point. I like it."

"See you, Sunday," she said, heading in. "Don't be a stranger."

"I'll be back when I run out of Red Cola."

The Glen Rose Sun Bulletin

Missing Fair Goers Appear on Road to Dublin

By Tom Tomland

NEWS STAFF REPORTER

A pair of missing Somervell County residents identified as Jessie Kinkaid (20), Roy West Carpenter (18), as well as four minor children whose names have been withheld due to privacy concerns, have been found, alongside dozens of others hailing from surrounding towns. Interviews with the once-missing individuals paint a harrowing, yet consistent account. All report the same tale of an eternal hell in the form of a dark carnival, somewhere below the dirt. Sheriff Bill Gustafson explained the testimonials as a case of mass delusion or "possibly tainted recreational drugs such as marijuana gummies" as likely culprits. Aside from undernourishment and mostly cosmetic injuries, all are expected to make complete physical recoveries, while the mental scarring will necessitate therapy. When asked to describe his ordeal, Teen Roy Carpenter stated, "I'm just glad to have my face back."

Our reporting is consistent with information coming in from surrounding counties. The Somervell Sheriff's Department will continue to brief the public as its investigation progresses.

Chapter Twenty-Three
Breakfast

S unday opened the door of the singlewide to let in the morning. Cool, crisp and golden. He carried a pitcher down the steps and gave water to his mother's flowers. If she ever did visit, he didn't want her to see them neglected. The daisies were thick and the little bee garden was buzzing. He even pinched a few buds from the knockout rose. Dead heading was legit gardener stuff. His mom would have been proud. Back inside, he went to the stove and fried up patty sausage, then broke four eggs into the fat, careful not to sully the yolks. The hashbrowns were store bought and warmed in the toaster. The coffee was burnt.

It was perfect.

He loaded up two plates and brought them outside just as Ms. Poppy pulled up on her Rascal.

"Right on time," he said.

She held up a bottle of Fireball. "You make coffee?"

"You know I did."

He fetched mugs and carried them to the little garden table his mother used to sit at to drink her tea. Poppy pulled the Rascal close and spiked her coffee. They ate without speaking, enjoying the quiet and the sun's warmth.

The inevitable holler of a Doucet broke the peace just as Sunday was sopping up yolk with his hashbrowns.

"Your mom could have held onto those little turds for us."

Sunday smiled. "I don't blame her for getting rid of them. You'd do the same."

"I would have put them in the *Skinner* and left 'em there."

Sunday chuckled. "I believe you."

"What'd the police say?"

"Nothing much they can do to me. Even Gaynes doesn't think I did anything. He's got a couple hundred formerly missing people claiming that Mom's been crowned the new queen of the twilight realm and responsible for releasing them from their bonds. I'm pretty sure I'm not the focus anymore."

"Nice to know she's thriving down there."

"Yeah. Seems that way. Miss her though."

"Me too." Ms. Poppy drank down half of her mug then shrugged toward the side yard of the mobile home. "That why you're hanging on to that old thing?"

Sunday considered the haunted latrine into which his mother had once disappeared. "She knows where to find us when she's ready."

Epilogue
The Twilight Garden

Minnie Alvarez, an eighty-one-year-old Alzheimer's patient at Bluebonnet Springs Senior Care, sat in the lunchroom not eating. She *was* physically hungry. In fact, her grumbling stomach prompted looks from surrounding patients, but she was too angry to eat. It was her well-trained manners that barely kept her from flinging her plate across the room.

She'd just gotten off a call with her grandson, Mateo, who had informed her that he was no longer going to bring by his daughter, Minnie's only great-great grandchild, to see her. She'd had a flare up the last time they'd visited and not remembered the girl. She remembered now. She remembered her most days. Her name was Vivica and she was a glorious, dark-haired wonder who could name every bird in the sky. Minnie had a picture of Vivica on her dresser in her room at the facility. Every morning, she looked at the picture and recited her name. She couldn't remember the last time she'd not recognized the smiling child.

But it wasn't just that she'd briefly forgotten Vivica. Apparently, she'd said some things she didn't intend to say. Rude, nasty things to Vivica and to Mateo. She understood that he was angry and why he was doing what he was doing, but she wasn't ready to lose her family. Not yet.

She tossed her plate, then promptly apologized and helped clean it up. It wasn't like her to lash out like that. Even if she felt Mateo had acted brashly with Vivica, he saw what was coming. So did she. More and more, the world seemed to change, where to everyone else it remained the same. Her mind was unraveling like a wind-beaten flag. Somedays she could *feel* it.

Back in her room, she cried. And then she was sitting in her chair with wet cheeks and not remembering why. She didn't need to remember to know she was sad. After a few minutes, she looked to her dresser and the picture of the little girl. Vivica, yes. Her great granddaughter, child of Mateo, who had decided she shouldn't see her great grandmother anymore.

Minnie groaned as she got up. In the bathroom was a stolen cafeteria knife that she'd hidden under her bathroom sink. Most of the memory patients had something sharp tucked away. There came a point that you wanted to go out still knowing who you were. That is, if you could remember you'd hidden the knife or whatever it was in the first place. Anyway, Minnie did.

She flipped on the light over the sink, then froze in wonder. She didn't remember hallucinations being part of Alzheimer's. She reached her thickly knuckled hand out to touch one of the beautiful blue flowers hanging from the vines that covered her walls. It was soft and cool and *real*. She opened her mouth and gaped. Few things left Minnie Alvarez speechless, but here she was.

The vines began to open, spreading apart in the place where her toilet had once been. In fact, the vines and flowers seemed to have erupted out of it and overtaken it. A woman appeared from behind a veil of honeysuckle. It was a shock, but Minnie wasn't the type to show it. She stood her ground. The stranger woman wore a radiant gown of flower petals. Sprigs of Texas Mountain Laurel decorated her dark locks and perfumed the air.

"Are you supposed to be God?" said Minnie like it was an accusation. "'Cause I haven't believed in that mumbo since Sunday School at San Miguel's Church in Laredo. And if you are God, you can kick pebbles."

The woman smiled kindly. Her eyes glowed warmly. "My name is Regina McWhorter. I used to live up in Glen Rose ... and I was like you. Memories dropping away with no warning, slowly losing myself."

Minnie reached out and touched the woman's cheek. She didn't flinch. Her skin was soft and warm.

"I can take you to a place where you'll stop forgetting. A place where everything you've lost will return." Vines crawled up the wall behind her. Blooms of morning glory twirled open.

Minnie eyed the sink and envisioned the tiny knife hidden beneath. Focusing back on Regina, she nodded. "I think I'll go with you."

Regina offered her hand and Minnie took it.

Quick Favor

Thank you so much for dedicating your time to reading this book! May we ask a quick favor?

Will you please take a moment to leave a review on Amazon, Goodreads, or wherever you purchased the book? Your words have power. Your review can help this book reach more readers. We appreciate you!

Acknowledgements

*S**hitshow* came about on a bike ride. I rolled past a port-a-potty and went, "Portal potty? Could be a story there." And here we are.

Thanks Dad, for reading and giving notes like you always do. I love sharing this experience with you. My friends Josh Rountree and Jamie Graham gave this story an early read and fantastic suggestions. L.P. Hernandez and L.C. Marino, the initials-monikered gentlemen behind Sobelo Books, were a pleasure to work with and provided edits that really made the thing pop.

For readers: I hope you had a fun trip. Thanks for lending your time to this story and have fun at your next county fair. Just ... go to the bathroom before you leave home. Love you!

Metal I listened to while editing this: Clown Core.

About the Author

Chris is an artist and writer living in Dallas, Texas, with his wife, daughter and a fluctuating herd of dog-like creatures (one is almost certainly a goat). He writes short stories and novels. *The Phlebotomist, Stringers,* and *The Redemption of Morgan Bright* are available everywhere.

Chris has also been a trial attorney in environmental cases for two decades. He represents people who have been injured, poisoned, or killed due to the conduct of others.

http://www.panatier.com

http://www.facebook.com/chrispanatier

Instagram: @chrispanatier

TikTok: @chrispanatier

Bluesky: @scribeofhades.bsky.social

Printed in Dunstable, United Kingdom

67094598R00122